# Hitching
## *the*
# Pitcher

Chevron Beautiful ©2017 www.barkercreek.com

# HITCHING
## *the*
# PITCHER

Rebecca Connolly
Sophia Summers
Heather B. Moore

Mirror Press

Interior design by Cora Johnson
Edited by Kelsey Down and Lisa Shepherd
Cover design by Rachael Anderson
Cover image credit: Shutterstock #531798565 by Alex Yakimovski
Published by Mirror Press, LLC

ISBN: 978-1-947152-57-1

## Belltown Six Pack Series

# HITCHING THE PITCHER

Sawyer Bennett has a secret. A risky thing, being one of the popular Belltown Six Pack, a group of six guys from the same college baseball team, all of whom got drafted and now play in the Major Leagues. Between the media frenzy over them and his bond with the guys, his secret has to stay carefully hidden if he wants it to stay that way. He needs to focus on his pitching and let everything else fall away.

Running into his former college girlfriend wasn't supposed to happen. Falling for her again wasn't supposed to happen. Confessing his secret to her was definitely not supposed to happen. But the harder he falls for Erica Moore, the more important his secret—and she—becomes.

# CHAPTER 1

COLUMBUS WAS COLD in February.

Not surprising, but practicing in Columbus in the cold might be surprising. Most teams had already gone to Florida or Arizona or someplace warm and temperate in the off-season.

Not the Black Racers. Not this year.

Toughening up, Sarge had called it. He was a militant sort of manager, hence his nickname, but it had worked for the team the last three years and would undoubtedly do the same this year. They'd head down to Arizona next week for a few days of warmer training before starting up some games, but until then, they'd be here.

Where it was cold and it was early.

Perfect for another sort of practice entirely—something entirely private.

"Ethics. Metaphysics. Epistemology. Logic."

The net of the pitcher's pocket didn't respond to the recitation of the four aspects of philosophy, but it did catch each of the four balls in varying aspects of the strike zone, which was good enough for Sawyer Bennett.

Didn't help him prepare for his History of Philosophy final, but it was good enough.

He walked down the stretch, gently shaking out his right arm to loosen it up, then scooping up the balls, shoving two in his pockets.

He craned his neck, wincing at the crack. "Logic. New and necessary reasoning."

He exhaled, sputtering his lips as he walked back to the practice mound, shaking out his arm again. "Consistency. Soundness. Completeness."

The unmistakable sound of cleats against concrete met his ears, and he clamped his mouth shut, clearing his throat when he reached the mound again, dropping the balls down except for one in his glove.

He listened for the cleats to go somewhere and heard the storage closet open and the cleats disappear within.

Must have been Gru, then. He was the only one who ever got here as early as Sawyer and was equally self-sufficient.

Sawyer looked down the stretch again, exhaling slowly, forcing away all thoughts but for the ball in his hand and the hours of studying in his head. He waited, then wound up.

"Aristotle," he grunted as he released the ball.

Strike.

He picked up the next ball and repeated his rhythm. "Pythagoras."

Strike.

"Thales."

Strike.

"Socrates."

Wild pitch.

Sawyer growled and cracked his neck again. "Stupid, stupid. Socrates didn't develop it; he used it."

"Who are we calling Socrates, and what did he use?"

Biting back a curse, Sawyer turned to face his teammate, punching idly into his glove. "Hey, Mace."

"Skeeter," Mace greeted, folding his tattooed arms and leaning against the cage. "Socrates. Who?"

"No one," Sawyer sighed. "Well, no, actual Socrates."

"What about him?"

Oh boy. Sawyer punched his glove again, fighting a wince. "He didn't develop deductive reasoning."

"True," Mace agreed with a nod, shocking Sawyer. "But his name was used so often in the description of it that it's a common misconception."

Sawyer blinked at the thick catcher, who was more likely to be found in a biker gang than behind a textbook. Or so he'd thought.

Mace grinned, his eyes crinkling as they usually did. "I was a philosophy major at Ohio State, Skeet. I know what I'm talking about."

Sawyer shook his head. "I can't see that."

"That's why I did it," came the quipped response. He cleared his throat and straightened. "All humans are mortal. Socrates is human. Therefore, Socrates is mortal."

Sawyer blinked again. "Uh-huh . . ."

Mace's eyes narrowed, arms still folded. "Which is an example of . . .?"

The panic known to every student in existence when called upon unexpectedly hit Sawyer square in the gut. "Uh . . . syllogism?"

"Question or answer?"

"Answer," Sawyer said quickly, scratching the back of his neck with his glove.

Mace nodded once. "Correct." Then his head tilted. "Why are you thinking philosophy while warming up? Without a bullpen catcher, I might add."

Sawyer chuckled uneasily, stepping off of the mound. "Just loosening up. Miguel wasn't here yet, so I pulled out the net. Used to throw to the net all the time as a kid. Kinda nostalgic, you know? No biggie. I only threw a couple."

"And the philosophy?"

He wasn't about to confess to his catcher the real reason, so he shrugged and lied. "Dabbling. You know what a head case I am."

Mace rolled his eyes, but he smiled. "Sure do. Come on, let's get a lap or two in before Gru makes us field his hits."

Grateful for a change in topic, Sawyer nodded and set down his glove, jogging out of the bullpen cages, exhaling a silent breath of relief. He'd have to figure out another way to quiz himself now, which would do just as well. He wasn't on this week; he could afford a little distraction at practice. Normally he was completely focused at all times, and he was teased for it, but off weeks were another matter.

He was way more human on off weeks. Spring training or not, he was glad for the off week, such as it was. There wasn't much by way of rest in the major leagues, not if one wanted to really make it, so taking advantage of what rest was available was a win. And perfect timing for a final exam, which was why he had scheduled it that way.

That, and a trip home.

Exam, then flight.

Back to Belltown and Belltown University, where, consequently, he could return the textbooks he'd ordered and pick up the next set.

Convenience was sweet indeed.

Provided he could get away from his family and the rest of the Six Pack, that is.

It could prove pretty challenging.

Every single one of them would have a field day if they

knew Sawyer was taking online classes. Rabbit might be chill about it, but none of the others would be. But they all had their degrees.

Only he had entered the draft without a diploma in hand.

That was public knowledge, and nobody cared.

But Sawyer did.

He'd made a promise, and he had to keep it.

Eventually.

He began to mentally recite answers in time with his jogging.

*Must. Eat. Everything. Pre. Performance. Says. Abba.*

*Milesian. Eleatic. Ephesian. Pluralism. Pythagoreanism. Sophism. Atomism.*

"Want help studying?" Mace asked casually as they started their second lap, nodding as other guys started following suit.

Sawyer side-eyed his catcher and teammate. "Studying what?"

Mace snorted once and wiped an arm over his mouth and neatly trimmed goatee. "Nobody dabbles in deductive reasoning, Skeet. Not even you. Not gonna ask questions, just offering to help. Got an exam?"

"Final," Sawyer admitted, dropping his voice although no one else was close enough to catch their conversation.

"When?"

"Tomorrow, I think."

"Not sure?"

Sawyer exhaled and saluted Sarge as they passed the dugout, the other guys doing the same. "Independent study. Just has to be this week."

Mace grunted. "And you're off to the motherland soon. Six Pack reunion?"

"Something like that."

"Kay. Tonight after film, we'll grab a bite, then come back to the clubhouse. I'll tell Jess not to expect me."

A twinge of guilt burst within him like a nasty bout of heartburn, and he screwed up his face in response. "Don't do that. I don't want you to upset Jess to give me philosophy pointers."

His catcher chortled a rumbling laugh. "You kidding? I'm antisocial, remember? Jess always wants me to get out with the guys and do something. She'll be elated. Done deal, Skeet. Be there, or be Pythagoras." He laughed harder at his own joke.

Sawyer, however, responded instinctively. "Developer of the Pythagorean theorem, fundamental rationale in Euclidean geometry. Had his own movement, and most commonly attributed teaching is metempsychosis."

Mace came to a stop as they finished their lap, not even remotely out of breath, and gave Sawyer a look. "Wow, Skeet. You're a mess."

It was true, and Sawyer was well aware. "I crammed last night," he admitted as he began to stretch. "Working on about three hours of sleep."

"Definitely don't miss college," Mace muttered, bending at the waist to stretch to the grass. "Well, tell Grizz I said hi. Dude still owes me two hundred bucks, so I'd appreciate it if you'd collect for me."

Sawyer barked a laugh. "Right, cuz Grizz is going to listen to me."

"Aw, Six Pack is Back Attack?" Remy crowed as he practically bounced towards them. "Need a groupie, Skeeter?"

Mace cuffed the eager shortstop, making their teammates laugh, including Remy. "No TV coverage for you, Remy. Make a few plays, and we'll see."

The ribbing went over well with the rest, and Sawyer felt

himself relaxing as they continued to warm up as a team. Baseball had always had a way of relaxing him, which was twisted as it was also his prime source of stress and anxiety. But it was his one true love, and baseball loved him in return.

Complicated relationships took work, but they could work well.

Or so he'd been told.

He'd endure the teasing and the questions and the envy of his teammates over a Six Pack reunion. He usually got that whenever they were brought up, mostly because the media tended to frenzy a little over their brotherhood. They hadn't been the best players drafted in their year, but they had all been drafted, and fairly early at that.

The name they'd earned at Belltown had carried over into the pros, and when they'd all moved up from minors, some sooner than others, things hit peak madness. Some of the guys loved the attention; some of them didn't.

But the Six Pack was special, and seeing the rest of the guys this weekend would be great. Being back in Belltown, and back on campus, would be amazing.

He'd have to rub the Lumberjack's boot, just in case.

He still had a few classes to go before he reached graduation, and with the season upon him, his focus would be limited at best in all things education.

But a promise was a promise, and Sawyer Bennett was a man of his word.

Sarge's telltale whistle pierced the air, and all of the players straightened from their stretches. "Batting," he told them all, his best drill-sergeant voice on full display. "Gru'll start us off."

"Not nice," Remy muttered as they moved in that direction. "Now we'll all look like crap by comparison."

"You always look like crap batting," Papa Jim pointed out with the crooked grin he was known for.

Sawyer laughed with the rest and pushed his educational thoughts out of his mind.

For the time being, at least.

Smaller airports were glorious things.

Albany wasn't that small, but it wasn't exactly a hub.

Either way, Sawyer wasn't recognized as he made his way to baggage claim, and there was something to be said for that. He didn't necessarily mind being spotted and spending time with fans, but it was also nice to get away from it. Especially when he was going home.

He wouldn't get away from attention at home.

But Belltown was different. They had seen him grow up, knew the scabby boy he'd been, and would remember every awkward school dance he had ever attended. He wasn't much of a celebrity there, though he did sign the occasional autograph and pause for a selfie every now and then.

Mostly from kids.

No one his age really wanted to talk to him, and most of the older generation didn't care.

It was the best.

He hefted his backpack more securely over his shoulder as he passed the line at McDonald's, pulling his faded Belltown hat a bit farther down, just in case. If he was right, and he usually was, his mom would be waiting for him with a small sign bearing his name as though she were only his driver. Her expression would be completely blank, but she would be fighting a smile the entire time.

He could only hope and pray that she wouldn't be in costume this time.

He'd never quite forgiven her for the Grinch ensemble three years ago.

Holding his breath, he rounded the corner and moved past TSA into the main terminal, his eyes scanning the few waiting people.

His mom was easy to spot: Belltown hoodie with a Lumberjack on it, hair pulled back in a neat bun, faded jeans, and her favorite, paint-splattered Keds. And there in her hands was the sign he'd expected.

This time it only read "Skeeter."

Sawyer exhaled with relief and grinned as he approached her, the blank expression staying fixed on her face. "Are you my ride?" he asked when he reached her.

"Are you Skeeter?" she retorted flatly.

"Could be," he replied. "What's for dinner in Belltown?"

His mom shrugged. "Not sure, really. Probably chicken and dumplings."

"That's my favorite. But my sister hates it."

"Then it's fortunate she's not coming until tomorrow." His mom's lips quirked, and her blank expression faltered as she fought a smile.

Sawyer laughed and stepped forward to hug her, the familiar embrace more of a welcome home than anything he would experience the entire trip. "Hi, Mom."

Her arms tightened around him. "Hi, sweetie. Welcome home."

He pulled back and looked her over. "Thanks for dressing up for me. Really. You shouldn't have."

She whacked him on the arm before slipping her arm around his waist. "I got up at dark thirty to get here since you insisted on an early flight instead of coming in at a regular human hour. You know full well how much I hate fast-food breakfast, and coffee before I have a decent breakfast to soak it up. You're paying for Sinclair's on the way home. You owe me."

"Yes, ma'am," Sawyer meekly replied as they made their way to baggage claim. "Three cake donuts with maple glaze, two bunches of classic donut holes, and an apple-raspberry bear claw. I'll even throw in a double-chocolate-and-cinnamon hot cocoa."

His mom nodded as though she'd expected nothing less. "With chocolate-chip marshmallows."

"Of course. After which, I'll drive you to the hospital for emergency treatment of your blood sugar and arteries and possibly a scan of your stomach."

"Never underestimate a woman's ability to consume chocolate and carbs."

"Put that on a bumper sticker."

A father and young son stopped on their way to security, their eyes on Sawyer, and the boy pointed. "Dad! Dad! It's Sawyer Bennett!"

"Shh!" the father hushed, putting a hand on his son's shoulder. "Scotty, it's not polite to point."

Sawyer looked at his mom, who was already smiling and nudged her head towards them. He returned the smile and moved to them, shaking hands with the dad firmly before crouching before the boy. "Hi there," he said, shifting into his greeting-fans voice.

"I knew it was you!" Scotty breathed, his eyes wide. "I have your poster on my wall!"

Sawyer chuckled. "Which poster, Scotty? Black Racers, Tomahawks, or Titans?"

"Six Pack," the boy answered.

That took Sawyer by surprise, though he wasn't sure why. He was, after all, only a short distance from home and the university. He was so used to fans from the majors, even those die-hards who'd followed him since minors, that he tended to forget about the hometown crowd and fellow Lumberjacks.

They were always, far and away, his favorite fans.

"Six Pack?" Sawyer repeated, sitting back on his heels. "Now we're talkin', Scotty."

"He's a Lumberjack at heart, Mr. Bennett," the father chimed in, putting a hand on his son's shoulder. "Knew 'Hail to Belltown' before he knew the alphabet."

Sawyer looked back at the kid with a smile. "My man." He cupped his hands around his mouth and called, "Timberline!"

Scotty immediately copied him. "Heave-ho!"

As one, Scotty and Sawyer drummed their hands against their thighs. "Ohhhhhh AND DOWN THEY GO!" they cheered together.

A few whoops and hollers echoed in the airport, and Sawyer laughed, his face actually heating with a strange sense of embarrassment. It was tough to explain the passion that Belltown instilled in him, and just how much being a Lumberjack had meant to him, but there was no denying it was still there.

And he saw the same passion for Belltown in the boy before him.

Grinning, Sawyer took off his hat, a classic Belltown number, and took the permanent marker his mom held out, then signed the bill before handing the cap out to Scotty. "Wear it with pride, Scotty. Represent."

Scotty immediately put that hat on his head and bent the bill just the way Sawyer and every other baseball player did. "Yes, sir. Thanks, Sawyer!"

"My pleasure. You ever get to play at Ackerman Field, you give me a call. I'll sit in your cheering section." He rose and nodded at Scotty's dad before putting his arm around his mom and continuing towards baggage claim.

"I love when you do that," his mom told him, patting his chest fondly. "Never gets old."

"I promise you it does," Sawyer countered. "But never with Belltown."

"Your dad would be so proud, Skeet."

Sawyer fought the urge to stiffen, swallowed instead, and pulled his mom in a little tighter. "Thanks. Now what's this Rachel tells me about you and some guy getting serious?"

The diversion worked, though it was obvious his mom wasn't fooled by it. She'd learned not to discuss her late husband with Sawyer, and she respected that boundary for the most part.

She probably thought it was too hard to talk about him, and she would be right.

But not for the reasons she suspected.

He was fairly certain she had no idea what Sawyer had promised him and what was going on within him as time went on and the promise went unfulfilled. He wasn't inclined to share that with his mom, and definitely not with his sister, and since neither of them had expressed strong opinions about his leaving school for the draft without a degree, he didn't feel the need to inform them that he was working towards said degree.

Sort of.

They managed to get his bags and get out of the airport without any further attention, and soon enough they were on the road towards Belltown. Normally he slept on this drive, but this morning he felt like watching. His mom chatted for a while, her usual eighties mix playing in the background, and he watched the scenery of eastern New York and then western Massachusetts pass him by. Familiar signs and sights made him smile, and he felt the familiar twinge of excitement coming home always gave him.

Then he saw it. The famous sign just outside of Belltown, hand carved and faded, though restored every two years.

*Welcome to Lumberjack Country.*

As per tradition, he rolled down his window, stuck his head out, and bellowed, "TIMBERLINE!"

His mother shook her head, laughing. "Sawyer Charles, it is eight thirty a.m. on a Thursday. You're going to wake someone."

"Tradition is tradition, Mom," he replied unapologetically as he rolled the window back up. "As is the drive through campus. Come on, let's go."

"You are so demanding," she complained as she turned towards campus.

Sawyer shrugged. "You're getting Sinclair's out of it, remember?" He looked back out at the approaching campus, smiling.

Then he sat forward, focusing on a lone woman walking out of The Glass Onion and turning to walk in the same direction they were driving. Dark hair, rosy complexion, brilliant smile, and startlingly familiar . . . He wrenched around to try and get a better look, but the road curved and it was impossible.

Surprisingly disappointed, he turned back around, scowling.

"What was that about?" his mom asked, giving him a curious look.

He debated his answer, then exhaled. "I thought I saw Erica Moore."

There was silence for a moment, and then, "I haven't thought about her in years. She was always my favorite of your girlfriends. What's she up to?"

Sawyer shook his head. "I don't know. We lost touch a while back."

"Oh, that's a shame. I wonder what she'd be doing here."

"Probably wasn't her, Mom," he told her. "Pretty sure she moved away."

"But her family still has the farm. I see Jean every now and then at the market . . ."

Sawyer let his mom go on, tuning out for the first time. He wasn't going to pretend to understand why he thought he saw Erica, or why he was disappointed he couldn't be sure it was her.

But disappointed he was, and his thoughts immediately filled with memories of her and of them.

Strange how welcoming those were.

Just like Belltown.

# Chapter 2

CAMPUS WAS BUSTLING, which wasn't surprising, and it made him even more relaxed about being there. Having picked up another hat from his childhood bedroom, dressed in a hoodie and jeans, backpack over one shoulder, he looked just like every other student there. No one would be looking at him, even in passing, as they would all be focused on getting to their next class or leaving for the afternoon.

He could wander his way around, relive the best days of his life, and enjoy the relative anonymity of being a Lumberjack amid thousands of other Lumberjacks.

And he intended to reminisce in full after he visited the bookstore.

The scores for his philosophy final hadn't come in yet, but he'd already received seven texts from Mace asking about it. And another three clearly intended to start a philosophical discussion.

Sawyer didn't care; he wouldn't ever need these books again, and he had no desire to ever think about philosophy again. He'd already registered for the next round of courses, and he was already thinking about those topics instead.

Well, considering them, at any rate.

In passing.

History of Sport would have some entertainment value, and Museums and Culture should be a walk in the park.

Neither fulfilled any sort of core credit, but he'd just done that with the philosophy class. He deserved something that would relax his brain rather than stress it, especially as they got closer to the season.

No need to pressure himself further.

He took a flyer from a group of girls handing them out, glancing down at it as he headed towards the bookstore.

Free cookies and milk at a meeting for a storytellers' club.

Once upon a time, he would have gone to something like that just for the free food and likelihood of cute girls. Being something of a celebrity had its perks back in the day, and the Six Pack had loved every second of it.

Maybe not *every* second, but certainly most of them.

He nodded at a professor he recognized as he neared the bookstore and opened the door, stepping back to hold it open for a young woman exiting.

"Thank you," she said in a familiar voice he couldn't place.

"You're welcome," he replied, smiling politely as he tried to look her over to help his memory out.

She froze, then looked up at him, and recognition dawned on him with the power of a jab to his solar plexus.

"Sawyer Bennett," she said slowly, her mouth curving in a perfect smile he recalled well, a slight dimple adding to the experience.

He felt himself smiling without any effort at all. "Erica Moore."

She laughed and immediately pulled him into a warm hug. "Oh my gosh! What are you doing here?"

Sawyer chuckled as he hugged her back; the scent of rose and honey filled his senses, almost nostalgic in its warmth. "It *is* my hometown, Erica."

Erica punched him in the arm as she pulled out of the embrace. "Mine, too, genius."

He rubbed at the sudden stinging in his arm. "Ow! Preseason, Teach! You'll ruin me."

"You'll survive," she muttered dryly, still smiling.

"And Belltown is not your hometown," he retorted. "You live in Mackenzie. Technically."

She skewered him with a look. "Home of Big Mack himself, which makes me more Lumberjack than you."

He gaped and gasped for effect. "Take it back."

She folded her arms and cocked a hip. "Nope."

Now Sawyer laughed and pulled her in for another hug. Somehow he'd forgotten how much he liked Erica as a person, and not just when they had dated. They'd been friends long before any of that, and good friends too. She was funny, she was fresh, and she seemed to find joy in simply living. And she was wickedly mischievous. At least a third of his pranks had been captained by her, though he would never admit that.

And he suddenly realized just how much he'd missed her. "Oh, it's good to see you, Teach. You haven't changed a bit."

"Same to you!" she quipped. She stepped back and tucked a windblown section of her long brown hair behind an ear, her bright-blue eyes nearly matching the sky above them. "Except for that. What is that?" She gestured to his chin.

He scratched at his well-tamed scruff. "What, this? It's attractive; everybody says so."

"Do they?" she commented with a raised brow. "Huh. I thought Grizz was the hairy one."

Sawyer scowled playfully. "He is, but that doesn't mean the rest of us are hairless."

17

Erica grinned and shook her head. "My gosh. What are you doing here, Sawyer?"

He jerked a thumb towards the athletic-complex side of campus. "Halftime of the game tomorrow. They're honoring the Six Pack."

"Are they?" She snorted in disbelief. "Nobody asked me. As the designated tutor of the Six Pack and company, I think I should have had a say in any accolades."

"Oh, shoot, I knew we forgot a name on the reference list when we applied for honors." He snapped in disappointment. "I don't know how we forgot to ask you."

"Shut up," Erica laughed. "I think it's great. You guys have really done it. You did what you said you were going to do, and you're all on great teams. Cole had a rough time last year with the Sea Rays, but they're supposed to be much better this season."

Sawyer stared at Erica in surprise, impressed and, he would admit, a little flattered. "You're following us? Where we're playing and how we're doing?"

She shrugged and stuffed her hands into her dark-green pea coat. "Nope. I just happen to keep ESPN on at all times, and the anchors seem a bit obsessed with you guys." She winked and smiled. "Of course I follow you guys! It's so fun! But I missed where you went after Orlando, and it's been a bit since I've heard your name. You okay? You're not hurt, are you?"

"I'm not hurt," he assured her with an easy smile, amused by the suggestion. "After Orlando, I got traded to the Black Racers, but they were in season and full up, so they had me train with their AAA team until they could call me up. I had a great time with the Rapids, and Missouri was a great stop."

"Black Racers?" Erica repeated, her brow creasing a little. "Columbus, Ohio?"

Sawyer nodded once. "Very good."

A quick smile spread across Erica's face. "I'm in Ohio a lot, actually. Sometimes Columbus, and sometimes Dayton. Like just an hour from you."

"Are you kidding me?" He shook his head in awe. "What in the world are you doing there?"

"Museum stuff," she replied with a faint toss of her hair. "I'm an assistant curator at a museum in Albany, but they have me travel a lot for special projects elsewhere. Gets me some decent exposure to other places, and I meet the best people. And special projects give me lots of interaction with the communities . . ."

Sawyer cocked his head, his smile turning quizzical. "You didn't go into teaching? I would have thought that was right up your alley."

She shrugged. "I tried that route for a while, but I couldn't get much. I teach some community classes when I can, and I head up the education department of the museum, not that it keeps me *that* busy." She rolled her eyes and laughed. "Actually, that's why I'm up here now. There's a teacher-training seminar here, and I'm hoping they let me become an adjunct professor. I've done it for a bit with a small New York school, so . . ."

"Need a reference?" Sawyer suggested with a grin. "As a former student, it's the least I can do."

Erica's smile turned knowing. "You were more than a former student to me, Sawyer. Always were."

Something in his chest tugged at that, and warmth slowly spread towards his face. "And I never quite saw you as just my tutor," he admitted candidly.

Her smile remained, and her eyes softened. "We did have some great times, didn't we?"

He nodded quickly. "We did. A lot of them." He cleared

his throat and straightened. "You going to be in town for a bit? The gang'll all be here tomorrow, and the boys would love to see you."

Erica nodded but then shook her head. "I'm here all weekend, but when I'm not at the seminar, I'm at the farm with the fam."

"Can't get away even for pizza with the Six Pack?" He was shocked at how much he wanted her to come with them, how much he wanted to see her again, to really talk . . .

Her nose wrinkled. "Don't think so. Meg's pretty set on taking all of my time. I wish I could, if that makes any difference."

"If Meg commandeered all of my time, I'd want to hang out with anyone else too."

"Stop," Erica groaned, tipping her head back. "You'll make me feel worse. And she's still with Jeff, so . . ."

Sawyer winced dramatically. "Yikes. I'll send Grizz out to save you. You know your mom always liked him best."

"Everybody liked Grizz best," Erica reminded him, still smiling.

"Even you?" he asked before he could stop himself.

Erica paused, then smiled with a distinctly cryptic air. "It was really, really good to see you, Sawyer."

He opened his arms and she stepped into them. "You too, Erica. So good." He held her for a long moment, and she let him, amazingly enough.

"I really am in Ohio a lot," she said quietly. "And my number hasn't changed. Let's grab dinner and really catch up, okay?"

Sawyer smiled and pulled back, giving her a thorough look. "Absolutely. I'd love to. And if you're ever in Columbus during the season, you'll find a ticket with your name on it. Good seats too. Promise."

Erica grinned at him, laughing. "Throw in a hot dog and frozen malt, and I'll come to every game."

"You're only coming for the food, aren't you?"

"Nothing like ballpark food at a great game."

"Hmm," Sawyer mused, looking up at the sky briefly. "Whoever told you that great piece of wisdom?"

Erica hummed nonchalantly. "Oh, just this really cute baseball player I used to know. Great on the field, lousy at chemistry."

Sawyer coughed a laugh as Erica backed away, wearing the mischievous look that used to be a favorite of his. "I got a B, thank you very much, and I ask you to name me one great player who really got chemistry."

She shrugged, still smiling at him. "I don't know, Axel seemed to get it just fine."

"Rude!" he called after her, only getting the sound of her laughter in response.

And then, for no good reason, he was laughing. Quietly but helplessly, and just to himself.

Erica Moore. His mother's favorite girlfriend, and, if he was being honest, his as well.

She'd always been his favorite.

Sawyer Bennett shook his head, wondered what in the world Fate was doing, and turned back to the bookstore to exchange textbooks, if not pick up some more Belltown paraphernalia.

He was growing fonder of this place by the moment.

"Shoo! Hah! Shoo! Hah! Shoo! Hah!"

The cheerleader standing on top of her male counterpart crossed her arms over her chest and began to fall backwards as the other cheerleaders beside her, mimicking a crosscut-saw team, dropped from their partners' shoulders to the ground.

The crowd and cheerleaders watched as the top cheerleader fell into the waiting arms of her teammates. "Ohhhhhhhh AND DOWN THEY GO!"

The buzzer sounded, and both teams returned to the court.

"Isn't it great to be back here? I freaking love this place."

Sawyer snorted a faint laugh and looked at Grizz. "We're down by five before the half, you hear the Timberline section cheer, and you get teary-eyed?"

"Heck yeah, I do!" came the heated retort from his friend, his dark goatee stretching with his grin. "No shame."

"Come on, come on, come on . . ." Cole hissed, his eyes fixed out on the court. "Campbell can catch us up if they'll get him the ball."

"Don't forget Richards," Ryker pointed out, arms folded as he leaned against the wall watching. "He's top of his game right now. His threes are amazing."

They all watched as Belltown marched down the court against Franklin, the ball passing easily between them before going to a lanky player who shot the most perfect three-pointer known to college basketball.

"Devin Richards!" called Ted Shanks, the traditional Belltown announcer, with all of the drama one could expect. "For the three!"

The crowd roared and cowbells clanged, the Timberline section on their feet, their faces painted in the school colors of red and blue, their flannel towels waving wildly.

Sawyer had to admit, even he was getting caught up in this now. Belltown hadn't made the conference playoffs in fifteen years, and now not only were they in them, they were ranked number two just behind this particular team. Franklin had been the reigning champs for five years, regularly made the NCAA tournament, and boasted a decent number of drafted players annually.

Belltown wasn't supposed to challenge them.

Yet here they were.

"Let's go!" Levi called, cupping his hands around his mouth. "Come on, boys!"

Axel looked up at the clock, grinning broadly. "Ten seconds. Make something happen . . ."

"TIM-BER!" the crowd chanted, clapping twice afterwards. "TIM-BER! TIM-BER!"

Just then, one of the boys intercepted a Franklin pass, darting back towards their basket.

The crowd roared its approval.

"GO!" Sawyer bellowed, clapping with the rest.

The ball was passed to another player, who looked up at the clock as he dribbled down the court.

"No fouls, no fouls, no fouls, no fouls . . ." Cole muttered, rubbing his hands together.

The player slowed his dribbling, gesturing to his teammates to slow, to hold, to wait . . .

"Four . . ." the crowd chanted. "Three . . . Two . . ."

He tossed the ball to Richards again, who jumped and sank another beautiful three-pointer just as the buzzer sounded.

The crowd exploded as the scoreboard shifted to show Belltown ahead by one point as they went into halftime. Players for Belltown hugged and slapped hands, rubbing the heads of the younger players, while the Franklin players jogged towards the visitor locker rooms with carefully blank expressions.

The band rose in their section and started playing the Belltown fight song, and the crowd began to clap in time.

Sawyer and the rest of the Six Pack joined in.

> *"Hail to Belltown, hail to thee,*
> *Proud and tall among the trees.*
> *Honor, glory, all be thine,*
> *Calling all to the timberline!*
> *Alma mater, we stand proud.*
> *Sons and daughters, rise up now!*
> *Hail to Belltown, hail to thee*
> *Lumberjacks, one and all are we!"*

Grizz elbowed Sawyer with a grin, and with every other Lumberjack in the stadium, the Six Pack cupped their hands around their mouths and bellowed, "Ohhhhhhhh!"

> *"Away we heave, away we hoe,*
> *We see and saw and down they go,*
> *Proud and mighty, strong and true,*
> *The Lumberjacks are coming through!"*

"Belltown! Belltown!" they all shouted, pumping their fists in the air.

> *"Ever grateful, ever there . . .*
> *We're Lumberjacks, the bold who dare!"*

Just as Sawyer had done in the airport with little Scotty, they all echoed the drumroll with a drawn-out, "Ohhhhh TIMBERRRRRRRRR!"

The percussion section beat out the remaining four beats, cymbals crashing each time.

Sawyer shook his head, applauding with the rest of Schubert Arena, grinning at the sight of the Belltown mascot, Big Mack the Lumberjack, coming over to greet them. The young man was burly, strapping, and sporting his very own rather impressive dark beard. Clad in the traditional flannel, suspenders, and cap, he twirled his axe on his shoulder, the traditional name carved into the handle.

Delilah. Bearer of luck, source of all Lumberjack power.

Thanks to the course he had taken two years ago called the Old Testament as Literature, Sawyer knew what an irony that was.

Benefits of education.

"The Six Pack," Big Mack said with a grin, shaking each of their hands in turn. "Big fan, guys. Great to see you."

Grizz shook the guy's hand hard, nodding in approval. "Definitely a better Big Mack than the one we had before we left. What's your pushup record, Mack?"

"Stop, Grizz," Ryker groaned. "Leave the guy alone, this is not a contest."

"Stay out of it, Rabbit," Grizz growled.

Big Mack was clearly not intimidated by the Major League status of the men around him. "Two seventy-four."

Axel muttered something in Spanish, rubbing his eyes.

"What Axe Man said," Cole agreed. "Grizz. Down."

Grizz laughed his booming laugh and patted Big Mack on the shoulder. "Heave-ho, my man."

Big Mack grinned. "Thanks, Grizz. Good luck this season." He nodded at them, then turned back out to join the cheerleaders.

"What about us?" Ryker demanded, flinging his arms out. "Come on now."

Sawyer shrugged and heaved a sigh. "Everybody likes Grizz best."

Cole snorted. "Says who?"

"Erica," he said before he could stop himself. Then he winced, knowing what was coming.

"TEACH?" at least three of the guys cried, turning to him.

He put his face against the cement wall. "Yeah."

The inquisition would begin in three . . . two . . . one . . .

"Ladies and gentlemen, please put your hands together for the voices of Lumberjack Radio, Dan Peterson and Pat Connor!"

The crowd roared, and Sawyer wasn't sure that sound had caused so much relief before, but it did now.

"Hey there, Belltown!" Dan called a bit too loudly for the microphone. "Thanks, Ted. Pat and I promise to keep this short and sweet so the LumberJettes can dazzle us all with their program, but first, we have something important to do."

"Yeah," Pat agreed, straightening his tie and grinning around at the crowd. "Some might say it's an honor. Not that long ago, Belltown did something pretty special. So special, in fact, that we made national news."

Sawyer groaned and shook his head. "These guys . . ."

"Give 'em a break, Skeet," Axel scolded, straightening his expensive suit without a tie and smoothing back his hair. "They don't get out much. Radio and all."

A few of the guys chuckled, and they all prepared themselves for their entrance.

"The Lumberjacks have always had an incredible baseball program," Dan was saying, "and our legendary coach, Rich Maxwell, is proof of that."

There was a pause for massive applause and whistles, which the Six Pack joined in heartily.

"The winningest coach in collegiate baseball history," Pat reminded them. "But even he had never done this before. We, the Lumberjack community, sent six of our finest and favorite baseball players into the Major League draft, and all of them got picked up."

"To honor our Belltown boys in this tournament," Dan continued, speaking louder over the growing excitement of the crowd, "and the Belltown boys we've sent out, here for you tonight we have Belltown's very own Six Pack! Ted Shanks, do the honors, please!"

The lights in Schubert Arena went down, and techno music began to play as blue laser lights and a smoke machine kicked on.

"Oh wow," Grizz murmured with a chuckle. "This is epic."

The music took on a more intense beat, electric guitars and drums kicking things up.

"Ladies and gentlemen," Ted announced deeply, "boys and girls, Lumberjacks of all ages, introducing your Belltown Six Pack!"

The arena roared in a frenzied pitch.

"Leading off, playing centerfield, number eleven, now playing for the California Sea Rays, Cole 'Big Dawg' Hunter!"

Cole slipped on his signature sunglasses—mirror lenses reflecting the upper lights—grinned, and jogged out into the arena, a spotlight following him as he moved to center court.

"Batting second, playing shortstop, number eighteen, now playing for the Seattle Sharks, Axel 'Axe Man' Diaz!"

Axel jogged out, earning some distinctly feminine shrieks as he did so, the spotlight entirely unnecessary but following anyway.

"Hitting third, the third baseman, number two, now playing for the Minnesota Ice, Levi 'Steal' Cox!"

Levi groaned and made a face. "Minnesota. It even sounds cold to say it," he grumbled before forcing a smile and running out of the tunnel.

"Sheesh," Sawyer muttered to the others. "He's not over that yet?"

"Nope," they replied together.

"Batting cleanup, playing first base, wearing lucky

number seven, now playing for the Baltimore Blue Jays, Ryker 'Rabbit' Stone!"

"Nice," Ryker said as the arena continued to roar, leaving Grizz and Sawyer in the tunnel waiting.

"I don't know about that," Sawyer commented. "A bit much, isn't it?"

"Come on, Skeet, this is great!" Grizz laughed.

Sawyer gave him a wry look. "Uh-huh."

"You're not off the hook about Erica, you know," Grizz told him as the crowd began to chant his name.

"Yes, I am," he shot back.

"Batting fifth, playing catcher, number nine, now playing for the Pittsburgh Knights, David 'Grizz' McCarthy!"

There was a huge rise in the crowd volume for Grizz, and Sawyer smirked.

Of course.

"No," Grizz told him, "you're not." He smacked Sawyer on the back before jogging onto the court, waving.

Sawyer scowled after his friend. "Yes. I am."

"And finally, our hometown hero, the pitcher, now playing for the Columbus Black Racers, wearing number twenty-one, Belltown's favorite son, Sawyer 'Skeeter' Bennett!"

"No pressure," Sawyer exhaled, smiling as he made his way out to center court, slapping hands with his teammates just the way they used to, including the chest bump with Grizz. He waved to the crowd, though he couldn't see a single one of them.

A highlight reel of the Six Pack began to play on the jumbotron above them, and for a few minutes, all of them were caught up in the nostalgia of their time together: old interviews, old teammates, championship moments, and even some especially ridiculous times that had somehow been caught on camera.

As the video ended and the lights went up, the band

began to play "Hail to Belltown" again, and they all joined in the singing and the clapping.

This time, as the crowd cried the usual call of "timber," the drums started another round of rolls, confusing all.

"Ladies and gents," Dan and Pat said together, "up in the rafters, to the left of the press box, we will forever honor our Belltown Six Pack!"

A banner was suddenly unfurled from the rafters, bearing each of their last names, their group name, and the number they had worn in college.

"Wow," Grizz breathed beside him. "Can I get teary-eyed now?"

The guys laughed, all of them waving to the crowd, but Sawyer, despite his teasing, found his own throat a little tight.

There really was no place like home.

# CHAPTER 3

"AND THAT SHOULD last us until next March, I think. The summer exhibit is still being considered, but I will send out a memo to all when the board has decided."

Erica nodded absently, not really listening but making notes on her tablet all the same. She was still mulling over the change in her life that had been reconnecting with Sawyer Bennett.

Sort of.

If seeing him on campus could count as reconnecting.

It certainly *felt* like reconnecting, but that could just be her wishful thinking. Which was a stunning idea: she actually *wanted* to reconnect with him.

Badly.

Who'd have thought?

She shook herself, tuning into the meeting briefly, relieved that, as far as she could tell, everything was the same as it had been the last time she'd talked with her boss. It wasn't unusual for her boss to change her mind over the course of twenty-four hours, or for Erica to suddenly discover changes in a staff meeting, but there was something rather refreshing about actually knowing what was going on.

What a concept.

A hand rose down at the opposite end of the table, and Erica bit back a groan.

"Yes, Jackson," Angela said with a careful expression, gesturing at him with her pen.

"Remind me what this summer's exhibit is," he replied, looking somehow smug and confused at the same time. "I've only just returned from my time at the British Museum, you know, and there has just been so much going on."

Erica closed her eyes briefly to save herself from being seen to roll them, and she suspected she was not alone. Jackson had been sent on assignment to the British Museum for a month, much to the envy of all the rest, and he never failed to remind anyone he could that he had spent some time there, "learning from the best" and improving his networking contacts.

Angela had privately confided that she had sent Jackson away for some peace and quiet, and for the sake of her sanity, not that the British Museum had actually requested one of her staff for anything.

Still, he was an excellent anthropologist, when he wanted to be.

"Native American Heritage," Angela informed him, absently tapping her pen into her palm. "We're in final discussions with several other museums also doing similar exhibits, and we're hoping to tie them all together in a series of sorts, something that will help each museum as well as increase awareness and appreciation."

Another hand rose, this one much more appreciated. "Kayleigh."

Kayleigh swiveled from side to side in her chair, as she usually did when she was thinking. "Shouldn't we touch base with one of the more culturally focused museums? Phoenix, I know, does an incredible job with theirs."

"Which brings me to my next point," Angela agreed with a nod. "We're sending an envoy to the Arizona Museum of the Cultural Arts for just that. Someone to ensure that our exhibits are accurate and appropriate, and to bring about more opportunity for future projects. And maybe even to get some of their artifacts on loan, if we butter them up enough."

A round of good-natured chuckling went around the table, and Erica shook her head, switching her tablet over to email for the time being. She'd only just finished managing a display on the history of logging and lumber mills, teaming up with several museums in Canada; there was no way she would be considered for the Arizona trip.

She was looking forward to a break, actually. Between being back and forth to Canada and the trip back home, she'd been living out of a suitcase for far too long, and her plants were more than halfway dead from her neglect.

Emails from shoe stores about sales, from Belltown U's alumni chapter asking for donations, from a few restaurants warning her that her perks were about to expire . . . She scrolled through them, deleting most without reading.

Junk mail took up at least a third of her inbox, sad to say.

"So we'll be sending Erica Moore as our envoy and exhibit ambassador."

Her name registered in her ears, but it took a moment for her mind to catch up, though her eyes had stopped focusing on her screen immediately. She looked up at her boss, her cheeks flaming as she reacted instinctively to being called on while not paying attention. "What?"

Angela smiled, and a few others laughed at her. "We're sending you to Phoenix, Erica. Numbers were up after your work on the winter exhibit, so the board was unanimous in sending you. You wouldn't mind spending a few weeks in a warmer climate, would you?"

Erica grinned, shaking her head. "No, ma'am, I would not. When do I leave?"

"I'll email you the details." Angela nodded in approval, then cleared her throat. "All right, moving on. Claire, what do you have for this summer's children's program?"

Erica let the conversation around her go on without really paying any attention to it. She kept a smile on her face, but her mind spun with the information she had just received.

Arizona for a few weeks at least. She wasn't opposed to heading out there, especially when it had been so cold this past winter, but she was exhausted. She was only an assistant curator, not even one of the full curators, and she was being sent out again.

On the plus side, being off-site meant she could devote more of her time to her online courses. There was a certain degree of freedom in being away from her official place of employment, and more often than not she was able to sightsee and relax while she was there. Or, in this case, teach.

It was strange, but her career was beginning to take her places, some of which were new and exciting, and yet all she really wanted to do was focus on those online courses and teaching. She'd give anything to run the summer children's program instead of flying here and there to collect and oversee and research. She'd hoped that her work on the Canada projects would give her that opportunity, but now . . .

Now it seemed she was doing such a good job in her current position that they were going to give her more responsibilities in that position instead of giving her freedom to maneuver.

Would it be too much to ask for time to reconsider her trip and for her to go back to Belltown for a weekend? She suddenly wanted to sit down with her mother across their worn kitchen table with a mug of cocoa and some molasses crinkles while they discussed important things late at night.

But she'd just come back from Belltown, and she highly doubted they would give her another chance to jet off like that. It was already halfway into February, and the pieces and displays for their summer exhibit needed to be set in stone as soon as possible.

Erica sighed very softly to herself and returned her attention to her tablet. She closed out of her email and opened her notes again, this time going to the notes from the teaching seminar at Belltown.

A wave of nostalgia hit her, and she found herself smiling without any trouble. It had been amazing to be back on campus, especially with all the excitement over the basketball team. The classes of the seminar had let out early to allow the attendees to go to the game if they had wanted to, and Erica would have given anything to be able to.

There would have been something so magical about being back in Schubert Arena and hearing the Timberline section and the band, to say nothing about seeing the Six Pack be honored.

And Sawyer . . .

She had so many conflicting emotions about Sawyer, about seeing him on campus and about not joining him and the guys at Mamma Sal's for pizza. She hadn't lied to him in any way; it *had* been really good to see him. Their relationship had always been one she looked on with fondness, the memories making her laugh more often than not. They'd been inseparable, or they would have been, had his schedule permitted it. Baseball was first in his life, and she had known that.

She hadn't expected him to break up with her over baseball, but there wasn't anything she could do about that now. It had been a straightforward breakup just before his senior season had really started, and the most uncomplicated breakup of her entire life. His regret had been clear, and his reluctance gave her hope, even though she knew how determined he was.

How determined he'd always been.

If there was one thing she could say she knew full well about Sawyer Bennett, it was that when he set his mind to something, he absolutely would follow through to the end.

Even if something, or someone, stood in his way.

At that time, it had been Erica standing in his way. Or so he'd claimed. She'd never wanted him to be faced with a choice of her or the sport he adored, and she'd never given him an ultimatum. She'd loved him just as he was, head case and baseball and all, but apparently he could not have more than one love in his life.

And that was that.

Somehow they'd remained friends, though their time together had decreased in frequency as the rest of the semester went on. When graduation had come, he hadn't been there, and it was only after the draft and the first documentary about the Six Pack that she'd learned he never obtained his degree. He moved away to start his career, and so did she.

She hadn't seen him since college—until the other day.

He looked good.

He looked really, really good.

And he'd hugged her really tight.

*Don't you dare,* her saner side warned. *Don't go there.*

She closed out of the seminar notes and went back to her emails, glancing up at the projector first to make sure she really wasn't missing anything in this meeting.

Scrolling through her inbox again, she found a message that wasn't junk at all, and her lungs cramped in an awkward way at seeing it.

It was from Sawyer Bennett, according to the email,

36

though she supposed an assistant could have sent it, if he had one. But the subject line read *Hey Teach*, which an assistant probably wouldn't have done, unless under instructions.

Which would be weird.

She opened the email, her emotions going off in twelve different directions, and carefully read each word.

*Hi Teach,*

*It was insanely good to see you on campus. All we needed was a stack of your pancakes and it would have been old times! The guys all say hi, and Grizz wants to give you a bear hug, so guard your ribs if you see him. The game was awesome, right? Can't believe we beat Franklin! What a night.*

*So I'm not going to be in Ohio for a while, and I didn't want you to think I wasn't calling on purpose. We're headed out to Arizona for preseason training and games. We play in the Cactus League, if you follow any of that. Should be good, I'll get to play Grizz and Rabbit while we're down there.*

*I lost your number when my phone busted some time back, but Rachel still had emails going back years. Of course, I had to tell her I saw you, and my sister turned into a detective. I'm sorry in advance if she gets to you. Call me if you need SWAT. 912-443-0218.*

*Don't give that out, or I'll call up Dr. Barnes and tell him about what really happened to your geology project.*

*Skeeter*

It would likely earn her some curious looks, but she grinned down at her tablet without shame.

Arizona? Right when she was going to Arizona? Granted, it was a huge state, so there was still the possibility that they would be ages apart from each other, but there was no reason she couldn't drive down to a game or two while she was there.

If he wanted.

He had said she should go to games in Ohio; why should Arizona be different?

She closed her tablet and drummed her fingers on the table, pretending at attentiveness for a minute, then pulled out her phone, typing in the number she had somehow already memorized.

*Hey Sawyer, it's Erica. Guess what.*

She was in love with her newly rented Arizona apartment. It was larger than her place in Albany and had way more amenities, not to mention it was perfectly located, fully furnished, and right across the street from a Mexican restaurant she was dying to try.

The museum had really set her up well this time. She might have to reconsider wanting to go into teaching instead of traveling.

She'd been in Arizona three days, and she had finally adjusted to the time change, though she still had some unpacking to do. The open-ended nature of her trip had her a little nervous, but considering she wasn't the one who had to pay for the airfare, or rent for that matter, she wasn't going to voice her concerns.

Her colleagues in Arizona were welcoming and warm, and they had given her a full tour of the museum and full access to anything she wanted. The exhibits were fascinating and pristine, and she'd gone through the entire place as a visitor first, then as a curator, taking notes as she went. It had been one of her favorite museum visits to date, and she was actually excited to get started.

The meetings didn't start until tomorrow, though, and even then, things were going to be so laidback that she was destined to have more free time than she had thought.

What to do with that?

Her mom wanted her to explore and send pictures and

videos. Meg wanted her to get them all some awesome cultural souvenirs, though she had yet to actually tell Erica what exactly she wanted. Bryant, her brother, wanted her to learn how to make what he called "legit Mexican food," which was laughable, as Erica was the worst cook in the family.

She would certainly find out which restaurants were the best, but she wouldn't be making anything. At all.

Especially considering she had been approved as an adjunct professor for Belltown, and her first classes started next week.

Classes. As in plural. She had been given *multiple* classes right off the bat.

There had been a pretty epic dance party when she'd received that email.

Her other classes she had been teaching here and there had wrapped up, so she had been able to apply for multiple classes from Belltown U, but she hadn't thought she'd get them all. Getting lessons prepped had been exciting and exhilarating, and she couldn't wait for things to start, though she knew full well that most of the students taking her classes weren't exactly going to be the dedicated sort. Some would be, of course, but her classes were fairly basic, which generally meant that students were only filling requirements.

Hard to be enthusiastic about a forced course.

She didn't mind so much. She was sure she could make the class entertaining enough to avoid being drudgery and useful enough to not be a waste of time. It was a fine line, and one she'd learned to maneuver well as a tutor in her under-graduate days.

The Six Pack had had quite a hand in tutoring *her* in that regard. Her teaching style would never have developed as it had if she'd had a different group of students, and for that alone she would be grateful.

The friendships she'd forged with them had been icing on the cake.

She missed that even now. But lines were drawn in a breakup, and out of necessity, the Six Pack had stuck together, as they should have done.

Still stung a bit though.

No relationship she'd had since had meant as much as that one.

No one else was Sawyer.

But even that relationship had ended, so she wasn't sure what that meant for her.

Her phone buzzed, bringing her out of her memories, and she reached for it, glancing at the screen briefly.

*Sawyer.*

"Seriously?" she said to herself, suddenly needing to swallow hard. She pushed the Answer button and brought the shaking phone to her ear. "Hello?"

"Hey," Sawyer responded brightly. "You here?"

Erica smiled and looked up at her ceiling. "Where's here?"

She heard him laugh once. "The Grand Canyon State, Teach. Glorious, sunny, non-humid, warm Arizona."

"Hmm," she mused, still smiling. "Deserty, dry, lots of prickly plants, and loads of turquoise?"

"That's the one. Know it?"

"We've been introduced." She sat back on her couch, tucking her feet up. "Barely."

"Great!" he said, and he sounded as though he really meant it. "You feeling like escaping?"

Erica chuckled, making a face he wouldn't see. "I thought I did escape. Isn't that what I'm doing here? And what you're doing here? Escaping winter, right?"

"Hey, I like winter," Sawyer protested. "I was fine with winter. Just makes it tough to play baseball, that's all."

"Ahh," Erica replied, nodding to herself. "That old thing. How is she? Letting you take her home yet?"

She heard a car door slam and some keys jangle. "Sure is! Haven't met her parents yet, though. Bit nervous about that one."

"You'll be fine, I'm sure." She shook her head, laughing. "How are you? Training okay?"

"Great, actually. Arm is feeling good, getting some good reps, and Sarge is putting me in for the opener against Philly. Nothing like starting things off for making an impression."

"That's fantastic, Sawyer! I'll have to come see it."

Keys jangled again. "I have your season tickets in my hands as we speak. Back to my question. You want to escape?"

Erica sat up, heart pounding. "And do what?"

"How long since you had amazing Mexican?" he asked, and she could hear the smile in his voice.

"Two days," she recited without shame. "I hit up a local place my first night in."

"Good girl. Meet me at this place called Casa Dea. It's in Tempe; I'll send you the address. The fajitas are legit."

Erica rolled her eyes with a snort. "Don't say legit. You sound like my brother."

Sawyer laughed, making her smile again. "Fair enough. It's very, very good. You coming?"

"Give me twenty minutes," she told him as she pushed off of the couch. "I'm in sweats."

"So am I," he told her. "Come as you are."

She looked at the phone as if he were crazy, then put it back to her ear. "No way. Twenty."

"Fifteen," he insisted. "I'm starving."

Erica sighed in exasperation. "There goes the makeup. Thanks, Sawyer."

"You don't need it anyway. Get going! See you soon."

He hung up before she could respond, and she just looked at her phone for a moment, completely bewildered.

What in the world was this?

Was she really meeting up with her favorite ex for Mexican on a whim?

They were less than half an hour from each other, and she had just gotten here. This could set a precedent. Did she want that?

She stood there in her sweats, chewing her lip for a long moment.

Then she bolted for her room, yanking her shirt off and rummaging in her barely put-together closet for something she could stand to be seen in.

Sixteen minutes later, she was walking into the restaurant at a brisk pace, slightly out of breath and, she was ashamed to admit, a little sweaty.

Dark shirts were a blessing in times like these.

She looked moderately cute, though Meg would have shrieked about her having black and brown in the same outfit. Considering she'd had almost no time to get ready and she had managed to get some basic makeup on and didn't look as though she were homeless, Erica was calling this a win.

She hadn't even seen Sawyer yet, and it was a win.

So far.

The interior of the restaurant was brightly colored with murals on each wall, sombreros and desert paraphernalia hanging here and there, and festive mariachi music playing over the speakers. There were a few guests in the place, and she scanned quickly for any overly attractive baseball players that might be hanging out in the vicinity.

It took a minute, but then she found one.

Just one.

He was poring over the menu, not looking for her, and for some reason, that was perfect.

That was the Sawyer she remembered.

She smiled at the hostess and told her she saw her party, and she headed towards the table. Sawyer looked up as she approached and broke into a wide grin that made her cheeks heat. He got up quickly, his snug Black Racers T-shirt riding up just a little as he moved out of the booth, and his dampened hair looked darker than its usual sandy color.

He opened his arms wide. "Erica!"

Gosh, he was good-looking.

She shook the errant thought away and smiled back. "Hey, stranger." She moved into his embrace, taking a moment to appreciate the fantastic smell of freshly showered man.

He pulled back, and she saw the faint edges of peeling sunburn on his nose and the outline of eye black on his cheeks. "You hungry?" he asked, stooping a little to look her in the eye.

Erica hefted her purse strap more securely on her shoulder. "Starving. Did you save me any chips and salsa?"

He gestured to the table, where a mostly full basket of chips sat next to two small dishes of salsa. "I did. It wasn't easy, but I managed to restrain myself."

She gave him a dubious look as she moved into the booth. "My hero." She picked up a menu, scanning it quickly. "You decide on anything yet?"

"Fajitas," he said simply as he sat back down, folding his hands on the table. "And a burrito combo."

Erica looked at him over the menu. "Don't they feed you on your team?"

"Not Mexican," he shot back. His attention shifted to just behind her, then he grinned. "Also, I ordered drinks for us."

"Oh yeah? What am I drinking today?" she asked without looking up.

Sawyer grunted once. "Same as always. Diet Coke with a lime wedge, water with lemon, both with minimal ice."

Slowly, Erica peeked over the top of the menu at him, unable to completely hide her shock.

He smiled easily. "You're very specific, Erica. Not hard to remember."

That was true, she supposed, but . . .

"Okay," she said slowly, folding the menu and setting it aside. "Let's try something harder. Order for me."

His eyes narrowed, but he inclined his head. "If you insist."

As if on cue, the waiter appeared with their drinks, setting them down. Then he pulled out a notepad. "Can I get you some appetizers, or are you ready to order your meal?"

"I'll have the steak fajitas," Sawyer told him with a crooked smile. "And the two-burrito combo with queso."

"Got it. And for you, ma'am?" he asked, looking at Erica expectantly.

Erica gestured at Sawyer, then folded her arms.

Sawyer sat up straighter and pulled the menu back out. "She will have . . . the green-chili enchiladas with pork, and how about a side of guac for the chips?"

The waiter looked at Erica for confirmation, and she nodded, smiling reluctantly. "He nailed it."

Sawyer pumped his fist, making her roll her eyes.

The waiter laughed and moved away.

Erica shook her head. "How did you know?"

Sawyer shrugged. "Lucky guess. I figured it was either that or the chimichangas, and you wouldn't have been upset with either."

"True enough," she admitted. She smiled at him and took a chance. "You look good, Sawyer."

He raised a brow. "Better than in Belltown?"

"Well, you're getting a tan," she pointed out. Then she gestured to her chin. "And this is gone, which is nice."

He rubbed his jaw. "I kinda miss it, but it's just hot down here. Fun, but hot. Speaking of . . ." He reached into his back pocket and pulled out an envelope, sliding it across the table to her. "Tickets."

Erica took the envelope and looked inside, several tickets within. She looked up at Sawyer. "Is there one for every game in here?"

Sawyer nodded. "Wasn't sure what your schedule was. Come when you can. If you want."

She did want. She very much did.

Touched, she tucked the tickets into her purse, her smile beginning to make her cheeks ache. "Thanks, Sawyer."

"Seems the least I can do," he told her, rubbing at his upper arm. "Considering I just found out you're teaching one of my online classes."

"I'm *what?*" she cried, laughing at his sheepish expression. "Seriously?"

He nodded. "Museums and Culture, with Erica Moore as my instructor. What are the odds, right?"

Erica took a chip and scooped it into the salsa. "This isn't going to get you a better grade, you know."

"I know," he replied, taking a chip himself. "But it doesn't hurt either." He winked, then laughed as he popped the chip in his mouth.

She shook her head, eating her own chip. "What are the odds?" she murmured, repeating his words.

"About the same as you and me winding up in Arizona at the same time, within fifty miles of each other." He quirked his brows, grinning again. "Meant to be, Teach. Just enjoy it."

"Uh-huh," she replied before smacking his hand away from the chip she wanted, making him laugh. "I better enjoy this food, too."

Sawyer grinned, reaching for a different chip. "You will. You'll enjoy both, I promise."

Erica returned his smile. "I think I will."

# CHAPTER 4

THERE WEREN'T MANY things quite like feeling exhausted and sore after a tough practice, especially when he knew he'd done well.

Today was one of those days.

Sawyer winced as he leaned back in the ice bath, the frigid pain one with which he was well acquainted—but that didn't make it any easier to endure. Panting in short, controlled bursts, he settled against the back of the tub, then groaned through clenched teeth.

"Baby."

Sawyer rolled his head on the edge of the tub to glare at Mace, currently getting his arms rubbed out. "Look who's talking. 'Ow, my arms hurt, can I get a massage?' Wuss."

Mace suddenly grimaced as the athletic trainer found a particularly tender spot. "If you think this is any more fun than that, you've got another thing coming." He groaned again and buried his face into the table, muffling curses.

Suddenly the ice bath didn't seem so bad. At least Sawyer would go numb eventually. He made a face up at the athletic trainer, who looked sympathetic but shrugged.

Treatment wasn't pretty, and it wasn't comfortable, but it did the job.

Mace heaved a sigh of relief and turned his head back to face Sawyer. "You were on fire today, Skeet. Philly's gonna have to watch out."

Sawyer grinned and motioned for an air fist bump, which was returned. "You too, Mace. Now if only I could keep my legs under me. Those drills were brutal."

The catcher shrugged as best as he could while being worked on. "Burned like Hades, but we'll be all right."

Sawyer nodded in agreement, closing his eyes and relaxing more now that the feeling in his legs was fading. "Good for us, right?"

Mace grunted in agreement, then said, "Hey, Kayla, doesn't Skeet need to ice down his shoulder too?"

"Yes, he does," the athletic trainer replied.

Sawyer's eyes popped open, staring at them both in outright betrayal. "No . . . Please, no. I'm in the ice! I'll put my arm in the ice! I'll go up to my neck!"

But the damage was done, and Kayla came over with several ice bags in her hands, strapping them on with her trusty roll of cling-wrap.

When his right arm was completely immobilized, bulky, and freezing, Sawyer glared at his snickering friend on the treatment table. "You'll get yours, Chuckles."

Mace gave him an appropriately innocent face. "I am only looking out for the welfare and health of my pitcher. It's important that you take care of that arm, isn't it, Kayla?"

Kayla nodded, her dark ponytail bouncing. "Sure is. Doc would insist, and you know it."

Sawyer turned his glare to her. "Did you draw the short straw to be in here while he supervises the rest of the team drills?"

She smiled with false enthusiasm. "Of course not. I love being in here with such cheerful athletes." Her smile dropped in favor of a complete deadpan expression, making them both laugh.

"Thank you for sacrificing, Kayla," Mace said as he sat up. "We like you better than Doc anyway."

Kayla rolled her eyes and picked up a pile of towels, moving into the laundry. "Uh-huh, sure, Mace."

Mace grabbed a band from the drawer beside him and moved to lie on his back, wrapping the band around one foot and stretching his calf with a grimace. "So once we're both feeling young and limber, and after we finish up team meetings, you wanna have one last night on the town? Jess flies in tomorrow, and that'll be it."

"Can't, buddy," Sawyer told him. "I've got something I need to do tonight."

His friend's brow wrinkled, then smoothed in an instant. "Ah. Start another class?"

"Shh!" Sawyer sat up in the ice bath, looking around, then made a pained noise as the cold reignited sensation against his skin.

"Ohhh," Mace said slowly, nodding in understanding, his sincerity not entirely clear. "I see. We aren't talking about this subject involving subjects. Well, have you plotted a new course on this deeply private escapade into educational endeavors?"

A chunk of ice flew towards Mace's head, but he dodged it easily.

Sawyer shook his head. "If I had my good arm . . ."

Mace continued to nod. "Right, Skeet. Right. Are you really not going to discuss it with me? I'm your catcher, man. Whatever is going on in your head, I need to know."

There was some truth to that, Sawyer supposed, however it might irritate him to admit it.

He leaned his head back against the tub. "I'm not missing going to the Gila Monster and eating Taco Joe's with you because of class. I promised a friend I'd show her around the area."

"You promised . . . Wait, what?" Mace raised his head from the table, the band snapping off of his foot. "Her? Who's her?"

"None of your business, that's who," Sawyer shot back. "She's a friend from college. We ran into each other when I was in Belltown, and it turns out she's going to be in Phoenix for a few weeks working."

Mace sat up and swung his legs off the table, wrapping the band around his other foot and stretching it out in front of him. "A Belltown babe? You kidding me?"

Sawyer waved a finger in the air. "They're called Lady Macks, you uncultured brick. The Belltown Babes are the tap-dancing squad."

Mace blinked. "I'm not sure I want to know how you know that."

"My sister is a dance major, dude. I know way more about the ins and outs of Belltown squads and traditions than I ever wanted to."

"Excuse me for being a Buckeye." Mace snorted and extended his leg further in the air, making a face against the tension. "So is your friend a friend or a *friend*?" he asked, his voice dipping suggestively.

"Interestingly," Sawyer said with a faint sniff, "I am, in fact, taking a class, though. Two, actually. Not sure how smart that is during preseason, but independent study, especially online, is fairly flexible."

Mace murmured a bland "Mm-hmm," that immediately made Sawyer suspicious.

"What?" he demanded, trying to decipher Mace's blank expression.

Mace grinned, his teeth flashing white in the midst of his dark beard. "The only thing more off limits than your academic hobbies is your friend. That's extremely interesting, Skeeter."

Sensing he was not going to win no matter which way this conversation went, Sawyer closed his eyes and began to hum "Hail to Belltown" to himself, using his free hand to conduct an imaginary band, though he had no idea how to do that. Waving his hand randomly in the air seemed close enough.

"I know you're avoiding the conversation," Mace told him over the sound of the fight song. "And if you think I'm going to let any of this go . . ."

"Ohhhhhhhh," Sawyer belted, plugging one of his ears with his free hand.

"There's a reason you weren't a music major," Mace called over the noise.

Sawyer went back to humming and conducting, tuning out his friend as best as he could.

Mace laughed, shaking his head. "Your evasion speaks louder than words, you know."

"Well, I think that does it for me," Sawyer said brightly, pushing himself out of the ice bath, his legs a brilliant scarlet. "Legs are golden. I'm just going to go change now and head out. Lots to do!" He hobbled towards the locker-room door, a bit wobbly on numb legs. "Belltown, Belltown!"

"Oh, come on!" Mace groaned from his table. "Finish the song at least!"

Sawyer stuck his head back around the shelves of therapy equipment with a crooked grin. "*Ever grateful, ever there . . . We're Lumberjacks, the bold who dare!*"

Apparently Mace knew the rest, cupping his hands around his mouth and yelling, "Ohhhhh TIMBER!"

"No," Sawyer scolded firmly with a shake of his head. "You aren't a Lumberjack. No rally cries."

The catcher rolled his eyes dramatically and shooed him away. "Go have fun on your date, Skeet."

Sawyer's eyes widened. "It's not a date. I'm being neighborly."

"Is she your neighbor?" Mace retorted with a knowing look.

Sputtering to himself, Sawyer declined to answer and turned back for the locker room.

Mace was an idiot. This wasn't even close to a date. He and Erica were simply spending time together, and he was helping her get acquainted with the area.

That was it.

It was.

"How about cereal? Do you have cereal?"

"Yes, Sawyer, I have cereal."

"What kinds? This is important."

Erica rolled her eyes for the forty-seventh time since they had entered the grocery store fifteen minutes ago. "Cheerios and Mini-Wheats."

Sawyer stopped the cart and stared at her with wide eyes. "Plain?" he demanded, evidently horrified by the thought.

"Oh, for heaven's sake," she groaned. "No. Honey-nut and strawberry, respectively."

His chest heaved on a massive sigh of relief, shaking his head. "Okay. Still, two boxes of cereal isn't enough." He pushed the cart down the aisle, eyes narrowing as he scanned the shelves. "Let's see. You like Fruit Loops, if I remember correctly, so we'll get those . . . Ooh, Frosted Flakes. Must have. No way! They have Berry Berry Kix!"

"Sawyer!" Erica protested with a laugh, tugging her long tee down a little. "Are you feeding yourself or me?"

He looked over his shoulder, a box of Berry Berry Kix in each hand. "Probably both. So what?" The boxes went into the cart, and he kept pushing on.

At this rate, she'd spend a month's rent on the food for a stay of just a few weeks.

Or maybe Sawyer would.

If he didn't calm down, she would absolutely make him pay.

What was initially meant to be a quick stop at the store before he showed her around town had turned into a full excursion to stock her entire apartment with whatever he thought necessary. She'd already gotten herself staples, but Sawyer didn't believe in staples alone, so crackers, peanut butter, spaghetti, marinara sauce, spices, baking supplies, and now cereal were coming home with her.

"Wait!" Sawyer cried, screeching the cart to a halt and turning to her with wide eyes. "We didn't get chocolate chips. Mom always told us to keep chocolate chips on hand no matter what."

"Life truth right there," Erica agreed with a nod. "Mamma Sal for the win. I'll go get a bag."

He snorted in response, adjusting the Belltown cap on his head. "A bag. Singular. Crazy. You need at least three. Emergencies happen."

Erica folded her arms and quirked a brow. "You have three bags of chocolate chips in your kitchen, mister?"

"Of course not," he scoffed. "I have five."

Her jaw dropped briefly, then she laughed. "Can you even make cookies?"

"I sure can," he shot back. "I'll bring you some next week, and then you are making me your mom's meatloaf."

"Done." Erica held out her hand to shake on it, and he took it.

He nodded at her. "Great. Now go get some. We have so much still to get."

She sighed in resignation and went back to the baking aisle for chocolate chips, snagging two boxes of instant chocolate pudding for good measure. Surely Sawyer wouldn't object to that.

Moving back to the cereal aisle, she frowned, finding it empty. Where in the world . . .?

She moved to the next aisle and found him dropping two cans of chili into the cart.

"Sawyer!" she groaned as she hurried to the cart. "Stop it. Come on, I don't need three months' worth of food."

"Who doesn't need chili?" he asked, resisting when she tried to take the cart from him. "We haven't even been to meat and dairy yet, let alone housewares."

Erica shook her head insistently. "I have chicken and ground beef already, and plenty of cheese, milk, and yogurt. Nothing left to get."

Sawyer made a face and leaned over the cart handle, his forearm muscles flexing just enough for her to notice them. "What about bread? Bagels? Chips? Popcorn?" He narrowed his eyes and smiled very slyly. "Ice cream . . .?"

She bit her lip, then threw her hands up in surrender. "Fine! Chips, popcorn, and ice cream. Then we are done with food, okay?"

"Ha!" He straightened and brushed imaginary dust from his shoulders. "Thought so."

"I hate you sometimes," she moaned as they began to walk again. "Seriously."

"No way, Erica." He gave her a sidelong look as they exited the aisle and moved towards their next section. "You love my enabling ways."

"Everyone loves their enabler sometimes," she retorted, slapping his arm. "It's why toxic relationships go on for so long. We don't know what's good for us."

Sawyer pretended to consider that. "But ice cream *is* good for us, right?"

"Right." She gave him a high five and draped her hand loosely at the edge of the cart.

"How about divide and conquer?" he suggested as they neared the chip aisle. "You run and get the ice cream; I'll handle chips and popcorn. Then we can go on to housewares."

Erica gave him a bemused look. "What do I need in housewares?"

He shrugged, making a face. "Won't know until we see it. But for sure a rug."

"A rug?" she repeated. "Why?"

"New apartment, you need a new rug."

"Do I?" she replied. "I had no idea."

He shooed her away. "Off with you now. Ice cream. Chop, chop."

"Now he's in a hurry," Erica muttered to herself as she did as he bid. Not that she needed much encouragement to go get ice cream, but Sawyer's behavior made it more enjoyable. The more she pretended to resist, the more insistent he became.

And she was really loving it.

She grabbed a half gallon of her favorite, rocky road, and, on impulse, Sawyer's favorite, chocolate chip cookie dough. She had no idea if he was on a strict diet, which he had tended to do when he was preseason in college, but if he was forcing ice cream upon her, she had no problem returning the favor.

Returning to the chip aisle, she found Sawyer on the phone, his expression not quite the cheery one she had left.

"Of course I knew she was dating. We teased her about it

when we were there," he was saying as he reached for a bag of chips. "She said there was a guy, but she never did get around to telling me . . . How long?" He waited for the answer, then covered his face with one hand. "Rach . . . Why wouldn't she tell us?"

Erica winced as she approached, holding up the ice cream when he met her eyes.

His expression didn't change, but he gave her a thumbs up.

She put the ice cream in the cart and took the handle from him. He let her, and he walked beside her as she moved out of the aisle and away from the food. "It's been five years; why would we have a problem with it? . . . Have you met him?"

Oh, this was not a conversation she needed to be hearing. However close she and Sawyer had been at one time in their lives, they certainly were not so now, and there was no reason to expect that they would ever be again. She'd been there when Sawyer's dad, Charlie, had passed away after a short and intense battle with pancreatic cancer, and what a toll it had taken on the entire family.

Ironically, and not surprisingly, it was just after all of that had happened that Sawyer had become so focused and determined in his baseball career. He'd always been dedicated, but never so desperately obsessed.

And now, it seemed, Mamma Sal was making some significant changes in her life.

Or had been, anyway.

"You're kidding," Sawyer breathed, making Erica look over at him and see how wide his eyes had gotten. "As in . . . *I've* met him. It's been years, but . . . Todd Landers, really? Do Tara or Millie know? . . . Right, you're not there." He ran a hand over his face again, then gripped the back of his neck. "Well, it sounds like I'll be calling Mom to ask some more questions." He rolled his eyes, a weak smile curving one side of his mouth. "No, Rach, I won't be rude. I don't even care that she is, I just wish she'd told us. You're not hiding a boyfriend from me too, are you? . . . Oh, good. Stay single, okay? Love you."

Erica pretended to be interested in the organizational bins she was currently passing as Sawyer hung up the phone.

"Sorry about that," he mumbled. "I never know what my sister is calling about, but . . ."

She shook her head immediately. "Don't even worry about it. None of my business."

Sawyer shrugged. "I don't mind you knowing. Mom's got a boyfriend."

"I kinda got that," Erica admitted with a smile.

"They've been together almost a year," he told her.

Now she stopped the cart and looked at him, gaping. "Are you serious?"

He nodded, then shook his head. "I have no idea how she kept that from us, or why. Rachel just found out because she basically interrogated Mom over FaceTime. Do you remember Tara and Millie Landers?"

Erica nodded quickly, pushing the cart forward again. "Of course. Tara was a star soccer player when the Six Pack ruled the world, and Millie came up after her, just as good. It's their dad?"

"Yeah. I didn't even know their mom had died." He trailed off, shoving his hands into his jeans pockets, walking beside her with an expression of shock.

"You okay with this?" Erica asked gently.

He gave a slow nod. "Yeah, in theory. Dad wouldn't want Mom to be alone, especially if she found love again. That's not an issue for me. I don't know if they've been serious for the whole year or if they were on and off, or . . . Why wouldn't she tell me?"

Erica paused to process her thoughts, then turned down the aisle of rugs and throw pillows. "You're a Major League baseball star trying to prove himself on a new team, and your sister is trying to break into the dance world professionally. Both of you require focus and minimal distractions. Maybe she was trying to spare you all that until she was sure it was something?"

"I get that," Sawyer said calmly. "But a year?"

"Maybe she took some convincing?" Erica shrugged and reached out to feel a patterned pillow. "I don't know, but I'm sure she had her reasons."

Sawyer grunted. "I guess. You ready?"

She nodded, and they silently made their way to the checkout. They tag-teamed loading the groceries onto the conveyor, and Sawyer surprised her by handing over his credit card to the cashier before she could even get her wallet from her purse.

"Sawyer," she protested, shaking her head.

He gave her a stern look. "Don't." He grabbed a Snickers from the candy section, and added that to the rest. "And the candy bar for my friend here."

The cashier nodded, smiling knowingly at Erica.

She had no idea how to respond to that. What did she think she knew? This wasn't . . .

This was . . .

Well, there was nothing to know, because Erica didn't know.

Sawyer put the groceries in the cart, thanked the cashier, and started pushing the cart out of the store. Erica trotted after him, tossing her purse over one shoulder.

"You didn't have to do that," she told him as they moved to his car.

"Sure I did," he replied without the same lightness from earlier. "You're new here. This is neighborly."

Was that what it was? Interesting.

Once the groceries were in the car, they took off towards Erica's apartment, Sawyer's rental car comfortable enough that she could nap in it if she wanted, but nice enough that she was afraid to.

Sawyer didn't say much as he drove, probably still mulling over his conversation with his sister.

There was no need to share details and thoughts with Erica, but the silence was unnerving.

She turned to look out of the window, watching the Arizona scenery pass without paying much attention to it.

Then something caught her eye, and she jerked to look back at it as they passed. She grinned and turned to Sawyer at once. "Was that a drive-in movie theater back there?"

He looked in the rearview mirror. "Uh, yeah, I think so."

"That is *awesome*," she gushed with excitement. "Whatever you're doing on Friday, cancel it. We're going."

Sawyer cracked a smile, which made her heart warm. "What if it's a terrible movie?"

"Then I'll buy you a cookie and make it all better," she retorted, undeterred. "Come on, Sawyer!"

He laughed and looked at her, his smile turning crooked. "Okay. It's a date."

They shared smiles, then Erica sat back and looked forward, her thoughts spinning.

A date? Like a *date* date? Or just a date?

Either way, a date with Sawyer Bennett had always been the best.

If she remembered correctly.

# CHAPTER 5

"DID YOU FIND out what's playing tonight?"

"Nope, and I don't really care. I'm just excited!"

"To watch a movie in my car? It comes with a DVD player, you know. I could pop in any movie you want and we could watch it in the comfort of your parking lot."

Erica slugged Sawyer in the arm with a grin. "It's not the same, and you know it!"

"Not the good arm!" he cried, batting her hand away as they pulled into the drive-in. "Come on, we start games next week!"

She rolled her eyes and reached into the tub of popcorn she had brought for a few kernels. "You'll live. Besides, aren't you already one of the starters?"

"Sure," Sawyer admitted easily. "But I'm new to them, remember? I got in for only three games last season, and a total of ten innings in the postseason. I have a lot to prove this year."

"You'll do it," she assured him with a wave of her hand. "Your two-seam alone should convince them, but if your cutter is still what it was . . ." She whistled and gave him a thumbs up.

He stared at her in disbelief. He knew that she had gone to most of his games in college, and she'd admitted to following the Six Pack since they'd left Belltown, but was he really to believe that she actually knew the ins and outs of the game? He knew for a fact that they had never gotten into the specifics of his pitches, let alone any other details of the game.

He wasn't sure she had ever been more attractive to him in his entire life.

He swallowed and forced a grin. "That's only two pitches."

Erica rolled her eyes one more time. "So toss in your change-up and a slider, just for kicks and giggles. How many different pitches do you need anyway?"

"Four should do it." Sawyer chuckled and shook his head. "Who taught you baseball stuff, Erica?"

"Axel." She smiled without shame. "I had to do something while you were taking extra reps and running more laps. We'd watch you practice, and he'd show me the differences in your pitches. He even tried to pitch to Grizz to illustrate."

Axel pitching? Sawyer snorted in derision as he pulled the car into an open spot. "*Tried* would be the operative word. Axe Man has a fantastic arm, but he can't throw a breaker to save his life. Needs a map to find the strike zone."

"Grizz made fun of him the entire time, no worries." She patted his hand as if to reassure him, then her smile turned mischievous. "And Axel said he pitches as well as you bat."

Sawyer exhaled roughly as though he'd been punched. "Oh, that's a low ball. Not nice. My batting average has really improved, I'll have you know."

"Well, there's only one direction it can go from where it was," she told him without emotion. "I don't think it goes negatively."

He gaped as she suddenly started laughing, and he

pretended to look around for any sort of support. "Who is filling your head with such lies? This is just uncalled for. I don't deserve to be abused in my own car on a date."

Erica barked another loud laugh and offered him the popcorn she was holding. "Will popcorn make it better?"

He scowled at her. "Maybe. But candy would give it a better chance."

On cue, Erica produced Gummi Peach Rings from her bag and jiggled them before him.

"Now we're talking!" he cheered, reaching for them. "I don't even care what we're seeing!"

"Good; I think it's a rom-com."

He froze in the act of scooping popcorn out with one hand. "Seriously?"

Erica laughed again, her blue eyes crinkling as she did so. "I don't know what horrified you more, the batting insult or the movie genre." She pulled her dark hair over one shoulder, absently brushing it a few times with her fingers. "No, I don't think it's a rom-com. I saw a sign that said it was classic movie night; you're safe."

Sawyer wiped at his brow in mock relief and turned the car off, sitting back and rolling down the windows to let the warm evening air filter in. It would cool off pretty quickly now that the sun was going down, but he'd brought jackets for them both, just in case.

He wasn't sure what had made him call this a date, but Erica hadn't denied it. And he didn't want her to.

Despite his arguing with Mace earlier in the week about just being neighborly and not dating, there was nothing to argue about here. This was absolutely a date, and he didn't mind admitting that to himself.

Dates were not commitments. They were not relationships, engagements, or promises. It was just a date.

With an ex-girlfriend who had been his favorite girl-friend and a close friend and someone with whom he would gladly spend as much time as he could.

That was all.

*Oh boy,* he thought to himself as the movie screen kicked on and the opening credits started. *This could get out of hand.*

But could it? Starting next week, his availability would be significantly compromised. It wouldn't be impossible to continue to see Erica, if she wanted to see him, but it would definitely get more complicated. His mind would be elsewhere most of the time, and he would have other responsibilities. Practices were tough right now as it was, but once they were starting games, he literally only had two days out of the entire preseason where he did not have a game of some kind.

Who would want to be limited like that?

"Ohhh," Erica said slowly from the passenger seat. "I've seen this one. It's one of my dad's favorites."

Sawyer glanced over at her. "Do you want to leave?"

She shook her head. "Nope. It's a pretty good one. And now I don't have to pay that much attention."

He nodded and tossed some more popcorn in his mouth. "How is your dad, anyway?"

"Fine," she replied. "Busy. They did well last season with the harvest. Farmers' markets always sell out of the jam, and Meg thinks we ought to try selling on a bigger market. She and Jeff are trying to get buyers interested, so that's got the whole family stressed. Bryant and Amy moved into the guest house last year with Livvy, and it's really helping to have Bryant on site. He'll take over when Dad retires, and Amy's about a step and a half behind Mom when it comes to the jam and pie side of things. Livvy's actually gotten really good about feeding the animals, which is great for a four-year-old."

Sawyer listened and noted the nostalgia in her tone. "Do you miss it?"

"Eh," she said with an indecisive head shake. "Sometimes. I'm not sure a farmgirl ever really leaves it, you know? I still help work it when I'm home, and I usually spend three weeks there in the summer to help with the orchard. I think I appreciate it more being away from it than I would if I had stayed."

"Were you thinking about staying?" That would have surprised him. As much as Erica had always loved her home, she'd also had some decently grand aspirations for herself that wouldn't have been particularly well suited to life on a farm, no matter how quaint it would have been.

Erica nibbled on some popcorn, but shook her head. "Nope. Dad offered, but I said no. I took a few business classes at Belltown out of curiosity, so I could have managed, but I wouldn't have liked it. If I didn't have a future brother-in-law who actually works in the field of business, I'd probably be the one doing all that. Thankfully, I do, so I'm free."

"Do you want to be free of the farm?"

"No, not really. But I don't want to be tied to it either."

"Fair enough."

They watched the movie in companionable silence, and it really was a fairly entertaining one, though it seemed familiar in a way.

Then it came to him.

"I've seen this," he whispered, leaning over. "We had to watch it for my Film in American Culture class."

Erica looked at him in bewilderment. "When did you take Film in American Culture?"

His cheeks heated faintly. "Last year."

"They offer that one online?" she asked, her gaze a little too questioning.

He managed a nod, returning his attention to the movie. "Yep. A little more required than the on-campus course, but they have movie nights at the Dav for those students. Those of us away from main campus have to watch them on our own."

Erica made a noncommittal sound. "I think I'd rather watch them on my own time than be forced into watching anything with a group at the Davisson Theater, thank you very much."

Sawyer snickered at that, remembering only too well how uncomfortable the ancient seats in the Dav were. No one enjoyed seeing anything there, he was sure of it.

"What else are you taking right now?" she whispered, fishing out chocolate from her purse. "Besides my riveting course on Museums and Culture."

"History of Sport," he whispered back. "I figured that would be an easier one to work with during the season."

"Depends on who's teaching it, I guess." She settled more comfortably in her seat, sliding her shoes off and tucking her knees into her chest.

He waited for more questions, and ones with a deeper inquiry behind them.

Why was he taking courses at all?

Did these courses fulfill any sort of requirement?

What did Film in American Literature have to do with anything?

Why hadn't he graduated?

She had to know he hadn't. It was everywhere in the news, or it had been at the time of the draft. Op-eds had been written about athletes turning pro without a degree, on both sides of the argument, and he was used as an example more often than not.

He was one of the only members of the Six Pack that hadn't done school talks. The other was Levi, and that's only because he refused all the offers.

It wasn't that Sawyer was sensitive about the subject; he was just a little defensive. Slightly aware. Insecure.

He waited.

She never asked a single follow-up question.

Sawyer stared at her in wonder. This woman was a born teacher, however little she was using those talents at the moment, and he had never met anyone that had been so dedicated to and excited about education. She'd singlehandedly saved the GPA of the entire Six Pack individually and collectively. When their professors wouldn't extend deadlines for them, she was the one who had vouched for the need, and never failed to succeed in changing their minds. The guys hadn't cared about impressing their professors; it had always been about impressing Erica.

He had sinned against every educational foundation she held dear, and she wasn't questioning it, offended by it, or, apparently, all that curious about it.

He saw her glance at him out of the corner of her eye, then return her attention to the movie. The tub of popcorn tilted invitingly in his direction without a word.

Forget everything and anything he'd thought about the difficulty of his schedule and any resistance against whatever it was he was doing with Erica.

He was all in right now.

He took the tub and set it between them, then reached over and took her now-free hand in his.

Erica didn't even stiffen. She adjusted her hold on his hand, then laced their fingers together.

A jolt of intense delight hit him in the gut, and it was all he could do to avoid exhaling in complete relief.

Then Erica reached into the tub of popcorn and flicked three kernels up at his face.

"Seriously?" he hissed.

"Shh," she scolded in all solemnity. "I'm watching a movie."

Hotchkiss Park was almost completely dark, which wasn't surprising, as all of the players and staff had left it several hours ago.

But that didn't stop Sawyer from pulling into the lot, turning off his car, and waving at Erica to follow him as he left the car and headed towards one of the doors.

"Normal people don't go into places once they're closed," she muttered to herself, shaking her head as she followed him against her better judgment.

The movie had been fun, but she could honestly say she remembered very little after Sawyer had taken her hand and after she linked their fingers. She couldn't have told anyone why she had done that, but she did know that it had been an instinct. Whether it was an instinct born of the habits of the past or one to rekindle whatever that had been, she really had no idea.

But she'd loved it.

Really loved it.

So when he'd asked if she wanted to go somewhere else when the movie was over, she'd agreed.

She hadn't thought they'd be breaking and entering the property of the Columbus Black Racers, possibly risking their freedom and spotless criminal records.

Who did this sort of thing on a date?

She pulled her borrowed fleece around her more tightly, taking a moment to briefly inhale the scent of Sawyer for good measure, in case they were shortly to be apprehended by local police.

He still smelled better than she remembered, and she'd loved to smell his sweatshirts then.

Sawyer stood by a door to the stadium, smiling at her in an unreadable manner.

She made a face at him. "Is this where you lead me into my life of crime?"

He nodded very soberly. "It is. And this is your initiation." He reached into his pocket and pulled out a key, handing it over to her with a bow fit for a butler. "Would you please commence with the breaking and entering?"

Erica took the key, then looked up at him. "Wouldn't it be trespassing?"

"It would," he conceded with another nod. "If I weren't allowed on the premises. As a valued member of the staff, technically I'm just coming into the office in my spare time." He flashed a quick grin. "Go on in. I want to show you around."

"Oh, so you're a workaholic," she replied, turning to put the key in the lock. "Everything makes so much more sense."

"That's me," Sawyer told her, holding the door as she opened it. "Working every moment I can. I was on edge the entire time we were at the movie, afraid I would enjoy myself and lose valuable working time."

Erica made a *tsk*ing noise as she stepped in, moving aside for him to lead the way. "I didn't realize you were paid by the hour. Who knew?"

He chuckled and took her hand, his smile turning more fond. "I forgot how much fun it is to banter with you."

Strange how such an odd compliment could make her want to smile hard enough to break her cheeks. She settled instead for rubbing her thumb against his hand. "So did I," she admitted.

He smiled at her for another long moment, then turned and began to pull her gently along behind him. "Okay, time for a grand tour, if you can bear it."

"And to our left . . ." Erica said in her best tour-guide voice.

"The left is nothing important," Sawyer corrected. "That's the janitorial closet. Don't ask me how I know that. But to our right . . ."

As he led her around, he could have passed as a decent guide for the tourists coming to Hotchkiss Park, if he needed a side job. But he was probably counting on her not knowing the historical facts of the place, and he could easily have been making them up. It would have been a very Sawyer thing to do, so she made a mental note to look into her local resources for fact checking.

Not to disprove him, but for her own information.

She was a nerd like that.

Eventually, the tour led them out to the actual field, which was almost enchanting by the light of a full Arizona moon.

Slowly, Sawyer led her down the first baseline, their fingers still loosely tangled with each other's. "How's museum stuff going?" he asked in a low voice.

She shrugged one shoulder. "It's all right. I honestly am not needed down here. The staff have everything so under control and ready for the transfer to our display, with notes and all, that I'm just superfluous."

"And what a lovely superfluous part you are," he teased with all grandness.

Erica curtseyed slightly. "Thank you, thank you." She rose and laughed a little before turning almost serious again. "I don't mind it, really. I wouldn't be doing that much back home either. At least here I feel useful. They're putting me on staff for their Kids Day coming up, so I'm learning the flow of the museum and the talking points. Apparently we get appointments from different classes in the area to come for a field trip, so we could get almost any age."

"That's great!" Sawyer said with real enthusiasm. "It would be like teaching for you, right?"

"As close as I'll get, yeah." She looked up at him brightly. "You know, you could use Kids Day for an assignment, if you wanted. Come through the tour and do a writeup. It should meet the requirements for one of the required papers."

Sawyer gave her a look. "I thought we weren't discussing our mutual class, Professor."

Erica made a sound of disgust. "It doesn't count if I tell you something that will work for a paper. You still have to go and write it, so maybe you'll do a terrible job and I can grade it accordingly."

He laughed and squeezed her hand. "Let me know when it is, and if it fits with my playing schedule, I'll come. And I'll write an amazing paper."

"See that you do," she replied with a haughty sniff. She hesitated, then ventured to ask a question she'd had for weeks now. "Why are you taking Museums and Culture anyway? That's a bit of a random class, isn't it?"

"Sure it is," came the unaffected reply. "But . . ." He hesitated, then stopped, looking down at her. "Can you keep a secret?"

She nodded immediately. "Sure can. I've never told anyone about Ellie, so . . ."

Sawyer grinned at the mention of his beloved classic car. "She's actually getting fully restored as we speak. We'll take her for a test drive when she's ready."

"Fantastic," she managed to squeak out without sounding too shocked. Was he saying he expected this, whatever it was, to extend beyond Arizona time and to involve trips home together?

She wasn't going to think about that. Not now.

Tonight in her bed, she would lose sleep wondering, but right now she was going to listen.

Sawyer started to walk again, rounding first and meandering with her towards second. "I didn't finish my degree."

Erica bit the inside of her cheek, then said, "I hate to break it to you, Sawyer, but that's no secret."

He squeezed her hand. "I know. But let's just say that it's been eating at me ever since. So I decided to work towards finishing."

"That's great!" she cried, squeezing back. "I know it might not seem necessary, given your current stardom, but I think you'll enjoy the security of it."

He nodded, though she wasn't sure he heard her. "So I've been told. The trouble is that my focus is elsewhere most of the time, so the more arduous classes wait until the off-season, but even if I just took the classes I need, I'd still be short total credits . . ."

"So you have to fill in with electives," Erica finished with a nod. "Makes sense now."

"Well . . ." Sawyer looked up at the starry night sky, slightly less brilliant due to the full moon, but no less lovely. "I may have already passed the necessary credit number. Mostly because I can't decide if I really want to have the degree I'm getting."

"Which is?" she prodded.

He winced, avoiding looking at her. "General Studies."

"Ah," she replied softly. "That does make things difficult."

Sawyer glanced down at her in surprise. "Does it?"

Erica was stunned he asked. "Well, yeah. It's so wide open, and a major like that is supposed to have an emphasis, and if you don't know the emphasis, how are you going to know what classes you want and need to take?"

"Exactly." He exhaled with relief, his thumb brushing against her hand warmly. "And then, I'll freely admit it, I avoid thinking about that by just taking whatever class looks good."

"Like Film in American Culture," she teased, elbowing him gently.

He nodded with a sheepish smile. "Great class, really. Didn't do anything for me, but I enjoyed it."

Erica leaned her head against his shoulder as they rounded second base. "That's good. I've never told you this, but I had a feeling you stopped enjoying college and your classes after your dad died."

Sawyer stiffened but didn't stop their motion. "I did. I coped with the loss by throwing myself into baseball. My advisor tried to tell me that I wasn't doing my degree any favors taking so many psychology and leadership classes, let alone the sports medicine and extra training classes. But I wouldn't listen. I had to be the best baseball player, the best pitcher, the best team leader I could be. That was suddenly what I was at Belltown for, not the education." He squeezed her hand and looked at her, his expression raw. "And not the relationships."

Erica met his eyes, squeezing his hand back. "I'm sorry I didn't understand that at the time."

He shook his head. "I'm sorry I couldn't explain it. And I'm sorry I hurt you."

How could so few words heal aches so old?

She smiled at him, a surge of tenderness swelling within her. If she'd had words, she'd have used them, but instead she leaned against him again, her free hand wrapping around his arm as she cuddled close. "Remind me. What are you taking right now besides my class?" she asked eventually in as normal a tone as she could manage. "I know you told me, but . . ."

"History of Sport," he told her, sounding like himself again as he leaned his head against hers. "Which, now that I mention it, doesn't have an iota of core value or program value."

"Eh," she replied with a shrug, feeling the tension that was still in him. "You're an athlete. What's a random sports class?"

He didn't need to feel guilt or shame or anything of the sort, not with her. He didn't need to explain himself and his decisions. They had different paths; that had never been in question, even when they had been together.

They'd only ever wondered how to make those paths run parallel, or at least meander in the same direction.

Which, as it happened, had led them both here.

And now.

"Well, I *was* taking History of Philosophy this past off-season," he told her with a quick sigh. "That was awful."

"Oof, yeah." She shuddered against him, distaste rippling across her skin. "Online would be so much worse than in class, and even that sounds rough. Did you ask Axel for help?"

Sawyer reared back in horror. "Are you insane? Of course not! We'd be discussing it for the next fifteen years. I'd never be rid of it."

Erica tossed her head back and laughed, clutching him for support as they reached third base and headed for home.

"You laugh," Sawyer protested, shaking his head, "but it would have been my life, and my curse. Thankfully, my own personal tutor happened to be our starting catcher, Mace."

"Mace?" she repeated, trying to remember the Black Racers roster, but failing miserably.

She'd only ever paid attention to Sawyer.

But he didn't need to know that.

"Mason Benjamin," Sawyer boomed like a sports announcer. He chuckled and resumed his normal tone. "Great guy, happened to catch me studying for my final and helped me prep. Got an eighty-seven percent, thank you very much."

"Atta boy!" she praised, patting his chest. "And what did Mace get for his troubles?"

Sawyer snorted. "Uh, my undying gratitude?"

"Boo. No." She shook her head for emphasis. "No. Bake him some of your cookies or get him a gift card."

"I can't bake my catcher cookies!" he sputtered. "He knows Grizz! I'd have to turn over my Man Card!"

Erica heaved a dramatic sigh. "Must be terrible cookies then. Pity. I've always found a man in an apron to be extremely attractive, and if he can deliver too? Mmm." She clicked her tongue, making the OK sign with one hand. "Money."

Sawyer cleared his throat. "Right. Wanna come over tomorrow and help make cookies? We can cook dinner too."

She smiled and nestled close as they reached home plate. "I'd love to, Sawyer."

He let go of her hand to put his arm around her shoulder and pull her even closer, and she reached up to take that hand in hers, tucking herself into his side. "Ready to go?" he murmured, his chin resting on her head.

"No," she replied. "No, let's go around again."

# CHAPTER 6

"AND NOW, TAKING the field, your Columbus Black Racers!"

The crowd cheered, though crowd was a bit of a generous term for the amount of fans in the stands. There were more coming in, of course, and the game was only just now getting underway, but there was always something to be said about a passionate fan base.

Today there wasn't much to say.

First preseason game, and this was how it was going to start.

Not particularly encouraging.

Pitching before a vacant ballpark was one thing, but what if this was their normal for the season? He always loved the energy of fans, and if they didn't have any . . .

What kind of pressure would that put on him?

What if he couldn't deliver?

"Don't do that," Mace grunted as he swatted him on the butt.

"Do what?" Sawyer replied as they walked out to the mound.

"Head games." Mace shook his head. "Don't do it. Come

77

on. Game one. Go time. We got these guys. Do your thing, and start us off. Your day, Skeet. Your inning." He held out his fist.

Sawyer exhaled, nodding, and pounded Mace's fist. "Yes, sir."

Mace gave him a firm nod. "Here we go, kid." He turned and jogged to the plate while Sawyer began his routine around the mound.

Circle once. Pause behind it. Crack his neck side to side. Exhale and drop the shoulders. Look at third.

Remy was ready for it, and he nodded back at him, punching his mitt eagerly. "Eyy, Skeeter, light 'em up, boy!"

Sawyer nodded in response, then stepped up to the rubber, exhaling again as he stared down at Mace.

Mace swayed his hips side to side, chatting up the ump and grinning at something he said. He mimicked tossing a ball at Sawyer, then squatted down behind home, pulling down his mask, swaying side to side as he waited.

Breathing suddenly became Sawyer's chief focus, and he turned as the batter came to the plate, the announcer's voice tuning out completely in his mind.

Instinct took over as his feet straddled the rubber, and his next routine began.

Left foot scratched in the dirt. Left again. Right. Right. Left. Right.

He looked at Mace, who signaled a pitch.

*Not for this guy.*

He shook his head.

Another signal.

*Yes.*

He nodded, then drew up, exhaling as he came set, the telltale pause that signaled the beginning of his pitch. His fingers glided over the familiar surface of the ball, stopping in the position they needed.

He wound up with an inhale, then released, the ball soaring down the field to Mace's waiting glove, the batter swinging too high for it.

*Strike one.*

The audience and his teammates cheered, the sounds barely registering to Sawyer as he nodded to Mace and caught the return throw.

"Again, Skeeter, get him again!" Gru called from second behind him.

Left. Left. Right. Right. Left. Right.

Look. Nod.

Come set. Wind up. Release.

*Ball one.*

Sawyer hissed, shaking his head to himself as the ball returned to him.

"Never mind, Skeet, never mind!" Papa Jim called from first. "Get him now, get him."

*Shake it off, Skeeter. Shake it off. Clean pitch. Clean it up.*

He scratched the dirt again. Looked.

*No. No.*

*Nod.*

He threw the pitch and grunted with satisfaction as it clapped against Mace's glove in the dead center of the strike zone.

"Eyyyy, SKEETER!" Remy hooted from third. "Nice one, Pitch!"

Mace pointed at Sawyer with a nod and tossed it back.

*One more. One more.*

He pitched, and the bat connected with the ball, sending it soaring over their heads.

Sawyer whirled, watching the ball fly directly towards center.

Creasy waved the others off, still chewing his wad of

Trident cinnamon gum, and caught the ball easily.

*One out.*

The park cheered, the fans beginning to trickle in more and more, applauding the beginning of the baseball season officially.

Sawyer exhaled, slowly shaking off the wave of nerves that were rippling across his skin.

Creasy tossed the ball to Gru, who tossed it over to Remy. Remy to Farrabee, Farrabee to Papa Jim, then back to Sawyer.

Sawyer looked over at the dugout, Sarge nodding and signaling his approval.

The bullpen had started the wave in his honor.

Morons.

Sawyer smiled at them, shaking his head.

First batter put away; he could handle this. Just a few more.

*Find your rhythm. Find the groove.*

*Heave-ho.*

The next batter came up, a lefty, and Sawyer grinned down to Mace.

He loved pitching against lefties.

Mace grinned back beneath his mask and gave the signal.

*Oh yeah.*

Three quick pitches, and he retired the batter without any incident.

*Two outs.*

The infield tossed the ball around again, then sent it back to Sawyer, whooping and hollering among themselves.

Sarge whistled and stepped up in the dugout, holding up three fingers with one hand and one finger with his other hand.

Sawyer nodded and looked down to Mace, who gave the accompanying signal.

This batter was dangerous, connected with the ball with ridiculous accuracy, and needed to have his potential damage minimized.

He also wasn't that fast.

Sawyer pitched a clean ball, which connected with power, veering deep right. He whirled to follow it and clapped into his mitt when Benji caught it without any difficulty.

"Yeah, Benj!" he whooped as they all jogged back to the dugout, slapping hands and rubbing the rookie's hair.

Entering the dugout, Sawyer let himself exhale deeply, grabbing a cup of water from the tray and sitting on the bench.

First inning pitched, and without anything to be held against him.

He could live with that.

"Nicely done, Skeet," Pickle grunted as he batted the brim of Sawyer's cap down.

Sawyer laughed and adjusted his hat back to look at the powerful left fielder. "Thanks, Pickle. Have fun."

Pickle quirked his eyebrows with a grin, his shaved head glinting already with perspiration. "Oh yeah. My year, baby."

"Your year for what?" Remy chortled, hanging over the railing to watch the batting. "Fashion icon of the year? Not with that tweed number you wore in today!"

Some good-natured ribbing continued in the dugout as Farrabee took the plate, leading them off.

Sawyer paid attention but stayed on the bench, leaning his head back to stretch his neck and relax as much as he could.

He'd woken this morning with excitement, energy, and anxiety, just as he always did. He'd had great seasons with Orlando and Kansas, but he'd been at the bottom of the pitching pack. Starting, but barely noticed.

This team, however, was different. He was fighting for

top spot and competing well for the position. His best chance for really establishing his name lay here, and it was best that he make a statement early on.

Right here, right now.

He nodded to himself and smiled when Mace sank down beside him, patting his knee proudly. "Nice three, Skeet. Let's do it again, huh?"

"You got it," Sawyer replied, taking a swig of the water again. "Let's go."

After the Black Racers failed to score a run, they took the field again, and Sawyer felt the comfortable familiarity of the pitcher's mound return to him in full force.

He struck out the next three batters without incident and returned to the dugout with high energy. Lots of high fives to his teammates, and, after getting two men on base and only one out, it was his turn to bat.

He approached the plate with determination, tapping his bat to his right foot as he walked. He adjusted his gloves, swung the bat up, shifted his grip, then stared down the pitcher as he readied his bat.

The pitch came, and he swung, missing easily.

"STRIKE!" the ump called.

Sawyer avoided wincing but exhaled through his nose as he readied again. He'd never been an amazing hitter, but surely he could get on base and advance his teammates.

He steadied himself and waited for the pitch, smacking the ball neatly between the right and center fielders. He made a mad dash towards first as Gru and Mace ran to third and second respectively.

Val, one of their coaches, clapped as Sawyer hit the bag, safe from being tagged out. "'Atta baby, nice hit, Skeet."

"Thanks," Sawyer breathed, shaking his head.

Val chuckled and patted his back. "Go ahead and lead

when you're ready, but not too far. Papa Jim's in a good mood; he should get Gru home safely, if not Mace. Just run like hell and watch Tiny, kay?"

Sawyer nodded once and did as his coach bid.

"How's the Six Pack, Skeeter?" the Riders' first baseman asked. "Saw the Franklin game. Nice touch."

"Doing fine, Kris," he returned, smiling a little. "Rabbit says hi."

Kris snorted and stooped, ready for the next batter. "Tell Rabbit I'll see him at the Derby and crush him."

"Noted." Sawyer dashed back to first as the pitcher threw there, then slowly started leading out again. The stands were way more full now, and he looked behind home plate as Papa Jim stepped away from the plate to adjust his gloves again.

Sawyer stopped when he saw Erica sitting there, her glasses pushed back on top of her head, wearing a simple gray T-shirt with print he couldn't see.

*She came.*

He didn't know why it was significant, considering she had said she would, but actually seeing her there . . .

Sudden pressure rose against his chest, tightening the muscles attached to at least six ribs, and his lungs couldn't seem to expand properly. His throat constricted, forcing him to attempt a swallow, which took three times to manage.

*Inhale. Exhale. Inhale . . .*

He shook his head and forced his attention back to the action on the field rather than the beauty in the stands. Papa Jim popped a ball to left field and got out, but he got Gru to score.

Remy struck out, ending the inning.

Up again, Sawyer moved to the mound, taking his cap and mitt from Farrabee as he ran them out to him before moving back to second.

He looked behind home again and saw Erica once more. She was looking right at him, and she smiled, that dimple appearing again.

He smiled back, then looked at the batter coming to the plate.

Right. Pitching.

Forcing his smile back, Sawyer waited for Mace's signal, nodded at it, then came set and pitched.

The ball soared and dropped behind second, Creasy scooping it up and launching it to Papa Jim. It didn't reach him in time, but at least the play ended.

Sawyer took the ball back and shook his head, looking at Mace again.

Signal. Nod. Come set.

Something in his periphery caught his attention, and he looked towards it instinctively, then groaned, making a face as the umpire called a balk.

The batter advanced to first while his teammate moved to second.

"Come on, Skeet!" Remy said behind him. "You got this, let's go!"

But what if he didn't? What if . . .

He shook his head, came set, and pitched.

Pickle caught the fly for an easy out.

Sawyer barely waited for Mace's signal for the next batter, throwing two balls before finally landing a decent ball, which was sent right into Gru's hands, and he tossed it to Farrabee, who sent it to Papa Jim for a clean double play, ending the misery.

He jogged back to the dugout, avoiding looking anywhere at all, relieved that he hadn't screwed up so badly it would affect the game's outcome.

But a balk? What was that about?

"Ey, Skeet," Remy said, slapping his shoulder. "You didn't look at me, man. You okay?"

"I'm not sure," Sawyer admitted as he descended into the bullpen. "I'm just . . . I lost my footing, and my head's not right."

Remy frowned and looked at Pickle. "Hey Pickle, you eat your eggs for breakfast?"

"Yeah," came the response. "You wearing your socks?"

Remy nodded and looked at Mace. "Mace? Skeeter broke his head. Fix it, man."

Mace sighed as he sank onto the bench, removing his catcher's gear. "Somebody walk under a ladder or throw some salt or toss up some Hail Marys so Skeeter can be absolved of his moment of weakness."

"Not funny," Sawyer retorted with a glare.

"Neither are bacon-flavored sunflower seeds, but I'm eating them anyway." Mace gave him a dubious look, then went back to his equipment. "Shake it off. Number four coming up. New inning, new set."

Sawyer nodded, feeling as though he'd been tutored again, leaning over the fence to focus on the game.

There was something so incredibly awesome about seeing a friend play a professional sport.

It was even more amazing to see that friend win.

Erica's seats had been fantastic, with the best view of Sawyer in action she could have hoped for. He'd done so well, pitching for five innings before the coach pulled him. She wasn't sure why he'd put in a reliever so soon, especially when Sawyer had been doing his job, but she had overheard one of the people around her explaining that it was too early in the season to play a starter to their absolute potential and that there was lots of time still for him to prove himself.

That had calmed her, and she'd been able to continue enjoying the game without worrying. The park was just as impressive in the daylight as it had been that night they'd been on the field the week before.

Not as romantic, but still pretty cool.

She wasn't sure where Sawyer's head would be at after the game, but in her mind, she thought he had every reason to be proud of himself. The bigger question for her was whether or not she should wait for him or just go home.

They had gone out a few times, but she couldn't exactly call that dating. She wanted to—would have loved to say such a thing—but couldn't.

They were friends, then.

With a past.

Oh boy. That wasn't something you wanted to tell people. No one asked as many questions when you were dating or when you could say the words *boyfriend* or *girlfriend*, but any mention of a past and you were trapped. Especially with the past they had . . .

She bit her lip, feeling the edges of worry creeping in. What was she doing? This guy had broken her heart before, and now she was playing with his very specific brand of fire.

*No,* she told herself. No, things were different now. It was okay that she was here, and she could absolutely play this cool. Old friends and all that. No one needed to know she was his ex-girlfriend.

Sawyer definitely wouldn't want his teammates to know, if they were anything like the Six Pack.

Would it have been better if she texted him to meet up later instead? That would avoid this whole potentially disastrous situation. But if she wasn't there after the game, when he had seen her in the stands . . .

Erica paced the parking lot, most of the cars already gone. She knew where Sawyer's car was. She avoided standing next to it, but from her current position she could see the door they had entered the other night. She would be able to tell very quickly what sort of a mood he was in, and if he might possibly want to see her.

Of course, it had been ages since the game had ended, and she was now completely starving, and she felt like an absolute idiot just waiting out here in the parking lot for a man she wasn't even officially anything to.

Minor details.

"What are you doing, Erica Moore?" she asked herself as she kicked a small pebble, wishing she'd painted her nails before putting on her sandals this morning.

She had no answers for herself, and none of the cars did either.

Useless vehicles.

The door opened, and, as luck would have it, Sawyer came out. She watched as he exhaled, his shoulders dropping, and he grinned up at the Arizona sky.

Oh good. He was happy.

Erica sighed in relief and started towards Sawyer, sticking her hands in the pockets of her jeans. He moved towards his car, and she headed that way too.

"Hey," she called when she was close enough.

He looked up in surprise, then smiled brightly. "Hey."

"You know where I could meet any really good-looking baseball players?" she asked with a wrinkle of her nose. "I'm kind of interested."

"Are you now?" Sawyer laughed quietly and strode over to her. "Well, I think a game just finished here, so if you hang around long enough, you might see one or two come out of the locker room."

Erica looked towards the door, clicking to herself. "I see. Anyone worth trying for?"

Sawyer shrugged. "The pitcher's all right. Not a great game, but decent enough. Some say he's not bad-looking, and I think he might be available."

"Oh," she said, feigning interest. "Is he a starter or a reliever?"

"Does it make a difference?" he returned.

She shook her head. "Not really. Just want to know if he's a man of power or endurance."

"Both," Sawyer said bluntly. "He's both."

Erica made a face, then shook her head. "Nah. I like catchers."

"What did that gorgeous woman say, Skeeter? She likes catchers?"

Sawyer rolled his eyes and turned towards a muscular man with dark hair and a leather jacket despite the heat of the day. "Go away, Mace!"

"Oh," Erica murmured quietly. "That's Mace? Good heavens, he could be Grizz's cousin."

"Don't encourage him," Sawyer muttered, taking her hand in his, linking her fingers.

Mace approached them with a broad smile, beaming through his neatly trimmed goatee. "Hi there. Mason Benjamin."

"Erica Moore," she returned, holding out her hand. "Pleasure to meet you."

"Likewise," Mace replied, sliding his eyes towards Sawyer.

"Great game," Erica complimented as she adjusted the hem of her T-shirt. "That throw to first in the eighth was amazing."

Mace grunted, though he smiled still. "Had to make Papa Jim work for it, you know. Prove the old man still has it." He indicated her shirt with a nod. "Great shirt. Love the classic Black Racers logo, right?"

"Oh, for sure, it is the best," she agreed without hesitation.

"Yay," Sawyer said dryly. "You're making friends. Good night, Mace."

Mace ignored him. "I take it I have you to thank for the plate of cookies Skeeter brought me the other day."

Sawyer muttered incoherently, looking away.

Erica grinned outright. "Well, the idea was mine, I'll admit it, but Sawyer made them himself. His mother's recipe. You are now sworn to never tell Grizz."

Mace held up three fingers. "Scout's honor. Besides, I'd have to tell him how good they are, and then he'd want some himself. Jess, my wife, refuses to let me have any more, yet she can eat as many as she wants. Very strange."

"That's a good rule," Erica pointed out. "I mean, you are technically in season now, and diet is everything."

"Oh, Jess will like you," Mace told her, nodding. He looked over at Sawyer. "Skeet, bring her over for dinner tonight, if you don't have plans. Jess wants me to grill, so if you just want to pick up some chips and some fruit to satisfy the aforementioned diet, it would be great."

Sawyer looked at Erica, and she looked at him. "You wanna go?" he asked.

"I mean, if you don't mind," she said hesitantly. "And if you want to. You guys did just finish a game."

"I'm going to be grilling anyway," Mace pointed out. "Whether you two are there or not. Might as well come. It'll be just the four of us, and maybe we'll put on a movie after dinner. Skeet and I will fall asleep halfway through, and you girls can talk about whatever you like."

Erica laughed and nodded. "I'm in if he is."

They both looked at Sawyer, who tossed up his free hand in surrender. "Fine, fine. We'll go. See you in an hour or so?"

"Perfect." Mace smiled at Erica brightly. "Jess will be thrilled. She says I'm antisocial, so this will get me off the hook for a month!"

"Glad to help," she replied, laughing.

Mace saluted and walked over to his car, leaving them alone.

"Sorry," Erica hissed, squeezing Sawyer's hand. "If you don't want to go . . ."

He turned to her and pulled her into a warm hug. "I don't mind at all," he murmured. "And it was really good to see you after the game."

Erica wound her hands around his waist and hugged him back. "I wasn't sure what I should do," she admitted. "But I wanted to see you."

"Good." He pulled back and smiled at her, making her bare toes tingle against her sandals. "Next time, I'll make sure you know where to go. Waiting out here is weird."

"Tell me about it," Erica said with a laugh. She gave him a careful look. "Good game?"

His face tightened very briefly, but then he nodded. "Good enough. Room to improve, but good enough." He squeezed her hand and turned towards his car. "Come on, let's pick up some food."

"Uh, my car?" Erica asked, jerking her thumb towards it in the visitor lot.

Sawyer waved that off. "We'll come back and get it after Mace's. Not going anywhere. I'll get you a parking pass too. My girl needs premium parking."

His girl?

Ohhh, her heart liked the sound of that.

It liked it a lot.

# CHAPTER 7

"DOES ANYBODY KNOW which tribe was most commonly found in the state of Arizona?"

A few hands shot into the air, and Erica smiled, pointing at one. "Yes?"

"Navajo," came the certain answer.

Erica nodded, smiling at the little girl. "Very good. Now does anybody know what sort of homes the Navajo traditionally had?"

The number of hands in the air decreased, and she pointed at one.

"Wouldn't it be teepees?" the boy asked, his brow wrinkling.

A little bit of chatter from the other kids seemed to ask the same, and Erica nodded. "Everybody seems to think of Native Americans in teepees, and some certainly did live in teepees. But the Navajo had homes that were called hogans. And they looked like this." She turned and gestured to a display behind her, which lit up as she turned.

The kids oohed and ahhed and moved closer to the display, where a manikin wore traditional Navajo apparel and stood outside of the structure.

The recording they'd finalized only that morning began to play overhead.

"The Navajo lived in a dome-shaped house made with a wooden frame and walls of clay," the deep male voice recited. "This was called a hogan. The door of the hogan always faced east to watch the sunrise."

The lights in the display changed to mimic a sunrise, and the kids reacted again.

Erica hid a smile and gestured to the teacher to move the kids down the line of displays, and the next recording began.

"The Navajo wore clothing made from woven yucca plants, or even deerskin," the recorded voice continued. "After they began raising sheep . . ."

"Now those are some fantastic displays," a familiar voice murmured behind her. "Someone is insanely talented."

She gasped and whirled with a grin. "Sawyer! What are you doing here? I thought you had a game in Glendale today!"

He chuckled and gave her a quick hug. "We do. They switched it to a night game, so I figured I should get some schoolwork done."

Erica snickered and pulled back to give him a scolding look. "About time. I'm still waiting for you to complete that first assignment."

He returned her look. "There's no set deadlines in independent study, Miss Adjunct Professor."

"I know," she laughed, swatting him. "Do you need some help with it? It's a bit of an out-there one . . ."

"What I need," he overrode gently, "is for my girlfriend to not worry about my educational endeavors. Especially when she's my teacher. Crosses too many boundaries."

Erica smiled and bit her lip, taking one of his hands. "Your girlfriend, huh?"

Sawyer gave her a crooked smile as his fingers played

with hers, his sandy scruff making him look almost rugged in his attractiveness. "I think so, yeah. If you're interested in the position."

If she was *interested*? She'd barely been able to think about anything else but him since they'd come to Arizona, and since they'd spent almost every moment together here . . .

Yeah, she was interested.

She made a face of consideration. "I think I could be persuaded to try for it. Any other applicants I should be worried about?"

Sawyer shook his head, his maddening, perfectly crooked smile still in place. "Not a single one." Then he paused. "Well . . ."

"Sawyer . . ." she warned.

"There is baseball," he pointed out. "She's kind of demanding. Likes to get in the way. Takes over a little. But just because I give her attention doesn't mean I feel any less for you."

Erica's heart fluttered, and she tipped her head back. "And what do you . . .?"

"Miss Moore," the teacher from the group called. "Where should we go next?"

"Oops," Erica whispered. "Sorry!"

Sawyer shook his head. "Don't worry about it. Go be teacher. I'll follow and take extra studious notes. We can continue this conversation when you're free."

"Thank you," she mouthed, darting back over to the group. "Okay, kids, tell me what you learned from those displays."

The rest of the Kids Day tour went off without a hitch, just as the three before it had, and Sawyer, true to his word, made a very studious observer. He hung back far enough to avoid being noticed, which was much appreciated.

She'd never be able to get the kids' attention back to the Navajo if they were obsessed with a baseball star.

Then again, from what she understood, the kids around here were mostly interested in the Arizona Falcons rather than the other teams who trained down here in the early spring, so she might have been safe.

Once the kids were safely involved in the more creative project associated with Kids Day, which was outside of Erica's responsibilities, she was able to sneak away and get back over to Sawyer, who lingered near the gift shop aimlessly.

It was amazing, but he actually looked like the baseball player he was even just standing there in jeans and a Henley. The baseball cap helped, sure, but his outfit did nothing to hide his immaculate build, and she suddenly flashed back to memories of him throwing strikeout after strikeout at Belltown. Her heart had soared with every one, and when Sawyer had showed any kind of emotion on the mound, she'd felt it. He was always so focused, so determined, that he was almost business-like in his methodology. The Six Pack had always been able to bring the best out in him, and every clenched fist and whoop of delight had brought back Sawyer's more human qualities.

And then, just a few weeks before his senior season, he'd broken her heart.

For baseball.

She'd never told him, but she had gone to every single game in spite of the breakup. She'd sat in different spots every time, never in what had become her usual seat, and she'd always left before the game had ended.

She couldn't lose that connection to Sawyer.

Then graduation had come, and life, and that had been the end.

Until now.

He wanted her to be his girlfriend, and she wanted to be.

But how long would it last this time? When would he get to overthinking and planning and strategizing and realize, yet again, that she was a distraction for him?

Could she go through all of that again? His senior season had arguably been his best, and there had been some small part of her that resented it. He *had* played better without her in his life, and there was the proof.

But that had been incredibly insecure of her, not to mention arrogant. As if she personally had had any influence at all on his baseball skills or career.

Second best behind a sport.

What if that was her permanent designation?

*Just because I give her attention doesn't mean I feel any less for you.*

She'd wanted to ask how he felt about her—she almost had.

She wasn't sure she wanted to know.

He'd never be able to choose between them, and she would never ask that of him.

Besides, she knew where the line was drawn, and where she stood in relation to it. She had the past to prove it.

Sawyer looked up and grinned, and Erica's knees went weak with longing.

Her heart turned over, but it gave her a sick feeling rather than a fluttery one.

She forced a smile and went over to him. "Whew, that was a rough one."

He shook his head. "You handled it like a pro. And honestly, you're a natural. I learned a ton! You can expect a very detailed paper from me, particularly on the quality of the instructor."

Erica rolled her eyes. "Don't waste space in the paper for that. I'll subtract that from the total length of the paper."

Sawyer chuckled and held up his hands. "Fine, fine, I'll pretend it wasn't you."

"That would be for the best." She bit her lip and wrung her hands a little. "You have time for a quick walk through the museum? Not the whole thing, but I just . . . I want some privacy with you."

He was instantly serious, his expression turning almost concerned with a line appearing between his brows. "Sure. Everything okay?"

She nodded quickly. "Of course. I just can't leave, and this is all very . . . open."

"Okay, sure. Lead on." He gestured for her, and she moved towards the pottery and artifacts exhibit, which should be fairly vacant on a Wednesday around lunch.

It wouldn't surprise her if she was completely wrong and it was packed, thus destroying any hope of having the private conversation she suddenly needed to have with him.

Thankfully, Fate was kind today, and it was empty.

Erica slowed her step and wandered along the arrowhead display, her eyes scanning absently over the edges of each item, taking in the description cards, and looking up at the map of Arizona indicating where each arrowhead had been found.

"Erica . . ."

She glanced over at Sawyer, who stared at her in expectation.

He shrugged pointedly. "What's on your mind?"

She rested her fingers on a case and drummed them lightly, exhaling slowly to herself.

She could do this. She could take steps towards preserving her dignity and preparing herself for painful possibilities. She could.

"Sawyer . . ." she began slowly, turning to face him fully,

her fingers shaking. "I'm not sure I'm strong enough to do this."

His brows rose just a little. "To do what, exactly?"

She gestured between them. "This," she said simply. "To be with you like this. Feeling what I feel. Again. Knowing what happened, knowing how it hurt, I don't know if I can bear it again if . . ."

"What if I told you I was feeling it too?" he told her in a low voice, stepping towards her. "That it feels better than before? That I'm terrified of letting you down again?"

Erica sighed, shaking her head and walking to him. "You didn't let me down. I understood."

"You deserved better," Sawyer insisted, and for the first time, she heard raw pain in his voice. "It was never about you, you know that, right? There was so much more going on with me, and I didn't know what to do, how to make it right. I was lost, Erica, and I thought . . . I thought I needed to remove everything from my life except baseball. It was not you."

"Yeah," she whispered, smiling as gently as she could. "I know."

Sawyer shook his head and closed the distance between them, taking her face in his hands. "I should never have let you go. I should have let myself feel this every day."

Her heart pounded furiously in her ears, and her fingers and toes were on fire. "Feel what?" she breathed, her cheeks flaming under his touch. "What is this, Sawyer?"

His eyes searched hers, then he slowly leaned in, then paused, waiting.

What did she want? To risk this again? To play it safe? He was giving her an out, and she could back away now.

The feeling of his hands against her face was heavenly, and the tickling sensation of his breath waiting across her lips the craziest tease in the world. His scent invaded her system and made her tingle all over, and a weak moan was rising in her throat.

She wanted this, after all that had passed. She wanted *him*.

And that was that.

Erica released a short, breathless sigh, tipped her head back, and pressed her lips to his.

"You swung like you were trying to beat someone! Or swatting a fly!"

"I did not. It was a great change-up, and that's all."

"The bat whistled as it cut through absolutely nothing but air." Grizz whistled faintly and waved his hand as though it were on a breeze.

Sawyer rolled his eyes and took an onion ring from the plate before him. "At least we won our game today. What was the score again, Grizz?"

Grizz mumbled under his breath, slouching and reaching for his glass, drinking as though it were something stronger than water.

Ryker shook his head with a wince. "I don't know how you guys made it into the postseason, Grizz. I've never seen a more unpredictable wild card than the Knights."

"We didn't get it either," Grizz admitted with a shrug. "The fact that we made it to the Series was miraculous. But we knew it was a fluke and wouldn't happen again, especially when Sterling, Jif, and Kiebler all left right after. I'm just biding my time."

Sawyer stared at his friend with interest. "Your agent got any tips for you? Anyone interested?"

"Oh, who knows," Grizz groaned, sitting back. "Preseason isn't exactly the time for feeling things out. Just gotta do my job and hope someone saves me. I'm open to offers, and he knows that, so we'll see. Pittsburgh's a nice enough city."

"That's what Rachel says," Sawyer added with a snort, taking a quick drink. "Though apparently lacking in real interest in dance."

Ryker flashed his usual grin. "Sis is in Pittsburgh? Grizz, why didn't you say?"

He looked at Ryker in bewilderment. "How was I to know that Skeeter's sister was there, Rabbit? It's a big city with lots of suburbs."

Ryker shrugged and dipped a fried pickle into ranch dressing. "Whatever you say, bro. A real friend would look after the sibling of a friend, especially in the Six Pack."

"Uh-huh," Grizz grunted, unconvinced. "And when was the last time you called my brother to check on him?"

Sawyer choked out a laugh. "Clint's a Marine. Rabbit's afraid of him."

"Am not!"

Sawyer's phone buzzed in his pocket and he pulled it out, glancing at the screen.

It was a text from Erica that read, *Tell the boys I said hi! Call me on the drive home!*

There was a heart after it, and for some completely stupid reason, that little heart made him smile.

"How's Erica?"

Sawyer jerked, his knee ramming into the table and making an extremely loud noise, just to make his embarrassment all the more obvious. "What? Who?"

Grizz and Ryker looked at each other, then back at Sawyer.

"What?" Sawyer said again, shifting his attention between them.

"Yep," Ryker suddenly grunted, sitting back and

reaching into his back pocket. "You're totally right." He pulled out a twenty-dollar bill and handed it over to Grizz.

"Thank you," Grizz quipped as he folded the bill and tucked it into the pocket of his shirt before folding his hands on the table and smiling expectantly at Sawyer.

Sawyer blinked. "What just happened?"

Grizz batted his lashes teasingly. "I just bet Rabbit here twenty bucks that you were seeing Erica again and that the text was from her. He doubted. Now I'm twenty bucks richer."

"Come on," Sawyer scoffed, sputtering in disbelief. "Why would you even go there?"

Grizz held up a finger and pulled out his phone, pressing a few buttons, then setting the phone down on the table on speakerphone.

It rang only twice. "Grizzy, what's up, pal?"

"Big Dawg," Grizz said, smiling at Sawyer slyly. "Got a hypothetical for you."

"Okay, shoot."

"Sitting here at dinner with Rabbit and Skeeter," Grizz said. "Say hi, boys."

"Hi," Ryker said cheerily while Sawyer withheld any enthusiasm.

"Hey uglies," Cole laughed. "Good games today. Nice swing, Skeet."

Sawyer threw up his hands and slumped against his chair. "Unbelievable."

"So what's the hypothetical, Grizz?" Cole asked.

Grizz cleared his throat and leaned closer to the phone. "Skeeter gets a text and smiles like a girl when he reads it. Who's it from?"

Cole scoffed loudly. "Come on, not even hard. Totally from Teach, man. Skeet, you two back on?"

"Thanks, Big Dawg," Grizz said before Sawyer could

push the End Call button. "I'll update in a bit." He ended the call and pocketed his phone. "Any questions?"

Sawyer looked at Grizz without speaking, his arms tightly folded and tension coiling inside him uncomfortably.

Ryker slid his chair back a bit and reached for his phone. "Right, Axe Man is next . . ."

"No," Sawyer said at once. "No. And not Steal either. You've made your point."

Grizz held out a hand to Ryker while still keeping his eyes on Sawyer, and Ryker slapped his hand before matching his expectant position.

Sawyer heaved a sigh and reached for another onion ring. "Yes."

"Yes what?" Ryker asked as Sawyer folded the onion ring into his mouth.

Sawyer chewed, shrugged a shoulder, then swallowed. "Yes, it was from Erica. She says hi, and she wants me to call when I drive back to Mesa."

Grizz rocked back on the legs of his chair. "And why would she want you to call?"

"Probably because she's my girlfriend, I don't know." Sawyer shrugged again, reaching over for some of Ryker's fried-pickle chips. "And I think she likes you guys. No idea why."

Ryker whistled slowly. "Girlfriend? That's more than just seeing her. Wow. Props, Skeeter. She's classy."

"Thanks, I think so," Sawyer admitted, raising his glass to clink against Ryker's.

"Huh-uh, wait a minute," Grizz said, bringing his chair back to its normal upright position. "She got back into a relationship with you after what happened with the last one?"

Sawyer looked at Grizz with a glower. "Yes. She did. We talked about it, and we're okay."

"Okay?" his friend repeated. "You told her why you did it?"

"I did," Sawyer defended himself, straightening up in his chair.

Grizz didn't budge. "All of it? Skeeter, we all knew what you were going through, and we were behind you a hundred percent, but none of us agreed with that breakup. She was your line to life outside of baseball, and you snapped it on purpose. We didn't say anything, mostly because you were an animal on the field and we loved that, but dude . . ."

Sawyer stared at Grizz, ready for something else to snap any minute.

"Did you tell her why?" Grizz asked again.

He'd never told the guys why, so how could he have told Erica?

Yet Grizz, for one, knew. And from looking at Ryker, it was clear he knew as well.

Did the others know?

What else did they know?

Did they know that he'd felt the weight of his father's death in more than just an emotional loss? That the burden of taking care of his family suddenly had fallen to him? He wouldn't have had the time to establish a career and get financially stable for his mom and Rachel, not with his degree and not taking the traditional path. Baseball was his one good skill, his only hope for actually becoming something in the world, and that was his ticket to being the man his father would have wanted him to be.

He'd had to devote himself to one thing and one thing only. Erica had been cut loose for the sake of his family, not just for his love of baseball.

Baseball had given him all that he'd needed to make sure he could take care of the family, if they needed.

Of course, it hadn't been needed, but at the time he couldn't have known that. His father had set everything up well for them, and there was no risk of them losing the house or anything else. His mom had gone back to work, and Rachel had earned a full scholarship.

By the time he'd realized the truth, he'd been drafted.

No, Erica didn't know that. Just like she didn't know the full truth about his efforts towards finishing his degree.

It was probably best that she not know just how many random sports classes he'd taken over the years, or how many flat-out random classes, just to say he was taking classes. No one, not even his mother, knew about the promise he'd made to his father, and so long as he continued to take courses in the general direction of finishing his degree, he had that connection and that promise.

When that was gone, it was entirely possible his father would be too.

Erica didn't need to know that.

No one did.

"Skeet?" Ryker prodded.

Sawyer looked up, unaware that he had ever looked away. "Yeah?"

"You zoned out. Did you tell Teach?"

He sighed and shook his head. "Not everything. I'm not sure she'll get it."

Grizz snorted once. "Of course she will. She knows you as well as we do, if not better, and we get it. Don't agree, but get it."

Sawyer hadn't considered that. He was positive his friends had wondered why he had acted so drastically about Erica back then, but Grizz was right: none of them had said a word about it. And they were not the sort of friends to protect each other's feelings. Instead, they had rallied around him and built him back up.

He had always said that at least half of the reason he had been drafted, and had been a player worth drafting, had been due to the Six Pack and all they had done for him.

And then there was Erica.

His connection to life outside of baseball, Grizz had said.

Did he have one of those?

Was it too late to get one if he did not?

He smiled to himself as he considered it. He was going to try for it, at any rate, and see where trying got him.

Surely anyone would understand that, too.

He reached for his glass and took a long sip from it, then looked at Grizz again. "By the way, Mace says you owe him two hundred dollars. Wants me to collect."

Grizz hooted a laugh and proceeded to tell Sawyer exactly what he thought about that.

None of which Sawyer would be repeating to Mace.

Ever.

# CHAPTER 8

"WAIT, WHY IS Sawyer in? He's supposed to be off today! Isn't Adam pitching?"

"He is, yep. Don't worry. Sarge apparently likes to mix things up. Since it's preseason, Mace says he wants to keep their legs going, even if the arms are getting a break."

Erica looked at Jess Benjamin, her new best friend, sitting beside her, wearing a ladies' version of her husband's jersey. "But left field?"

Jess grinned with her perfect teeth, her long auburn hair hanging in a ponytail through the back of her cap. "Sawyer's a good athlete. He can do it."

"I know he *can* do it," Erica pointed out, shaking her head as she looked back out onto the field where her boyfriend was now standing. "But it doesn't necessarily mean that he *should.*"

"True!" Jess laughed. She patted Erica's shoulder. "Don't worry; Sarge wouldn't put him in unless he was confident, and Damien wouldn't have let Sarge put him in if he thought Sawyer needed more rest."

Erica nodded without really answering. She supposed

that was true, from what she had heard of Damien, the pitching coach. He tended to be fairly protective of his guys even if Sarge wanted them.

If both of them thought Sawyer could handle left field . . .

She gasped as a ball popped high towards left field, and she clenched her fists and her teeth. "Come on, baby, come on . . ." she hissed, tracking the distance between the ball and Sawyer's glove.

He caught it easily, and the jumbotron showed his broad, crooked grin as he threw the ball to Farrabee. The dugout and bullpen whooped and hollered, and Sawyer blew them a kiss.

"Someone is pleased with himself," Jess said with a hearty laugh as she applauded.

"Idiot," Erica muttered, sitting back hard against her seat. "Only two more outs and one more inning to go."

Jess patted her again. "He won't keep him in the whole game. And look, Sawyer's better than a youth-league player. Even he can catch a fly ball. I promise, he's fine."

*Unless something goes wrong,* Erica thought to herself.

If there was one thing she knew about Sawyer Bennett it was that as hard as he trained, it was never good enough. He held himself to incredibly strenuous standards, and any error on his part would lead to hours of regret and blame, which would lead to even more hours of increased training.

If he ever felt that he was letting his team down, he would spiral so quickly it would be next to impossible to reason with him.

"Skeeter's a headcase," Levi Cox had told her back in their Belltown days, when she had been their tutor. "You get used to it."

She'd thought that was simply a teasing remark from a friend, but it turned out to be true. Sawyer was overanalytical, overcommitted, and underequipped with appropriate coping mechanisms for the results of his overanalyzing and overcommitting. She'd considered sports psychology as a major after seeing Sawyer's struggles firsthand, but she'd decided— probably for the best—to leave that world to others with less emotional ties.

As she understood it, he had taken sports psych classes, but she was willing to bet that had been more to get his head focused for pitching and games and possibly for leading his team—and less for everything else.

The things that he would really need those skills for.

Details.

"Let Sawyer have some fun, Erica," Jess murmured, squeezing her arm. "Trust me, I know more about what you're worried about than you think."

Erica looked at her friend, searching the green eyes for understanding and actually finding it there.

Realization dawned, and Erica smiled with relief she hadn't known she needed to feel. "Right. Mace, huh?"

"Mmhmm," Jess said with a nod. "He keeps tabs on all his pitchers, but he seems to take a special interest in Sawyer. Sees him like a little brother."

Erica laughed once. "Don't tell Sawyer that! He thinks he's the dad of the team."

Jess gave her a bewildered look. "With Papa Jim on the team? Seriously?"

Erica shrugged, laughing again. "I didn't say it made any sense. It's just the fact of the thing."

"Boys and baseball," Jess said fondly almost to herself, shaking her head.

Erica nodded in agreement as they returned to watching the rest of the inning. Sawyer didn't have to do much, but he seemed to love just being out there on the field in any capacity.

It was great to see him so relaxed and enjoying himself. He loved baseball, beyond his personal dedication to it, and towards the end of his college career, she hadn't been sure he was having as much fun with it as he once might have. The Six Pack helped things, absolutely, but it had still become an obsession.

Out there, at this moment, this might have been a pickup game with the Six Pack, where the losers bought pizza for the winners.

There was something to be said for that.

Erica looked up at the score as the Black Racers returned to the dugout to bat again. "Well, I suppose we are ahead by three runs, so there is a little wiggle room."

"Stop worrying, Erica," Jess insisted, waving a dismissive hand as she sat back and crossed an ankle over her knee. "Sawyer will be flying high after this game, you'll see."

"I know," she murmured, craning to try and see into the dugout. "He'll be fine until he pitches again in a few days. Then he'll go all silent and brooding and watch too much film . . . They're playing the Blue Jays on his next day, so he'll have to go up against Ryker."

Jess hissed a little, making a face. "Ryker had a good season last year." Then she grinned outright. "Do they still have that Six Pack bet going on? You know, if Skeeter strikes out Ryker, Ryker has to do something?"

Erica glanced at Jess in thought, then shook her head. "I have no idea. They didn't do that when I knew them at Belltown, obviously, and since then . . . Well, I don't know."

"Find out," her friend insisted. "If Ryker gets a piece of Sawyer's fastball, not that I would ever root for any such thing, I'm going to want my camera out after the game."

That seemed strange, and Erica frowned. "Why? What's the forfeit?"

Jess blinked, then her brow furrowed. "Have you ever paid attention to when they play each other?"

Erica shrugged. "I followed the scores . . ."

A slow smile spread across Jess's face, her freckled cheeks crinkling with it. "Oh, Erica . . . This is going to be so good."

"Why?" Erica asked, still completely lost. "What do they do?"

Jess just shook her head. "When you get home tonight, look it up. If you know the guys as well as you think, you'll have no problem believing what they're capable of."

That was a horrifying thought.

At Belltown alone the Six Pack had been capable of mischief beyond belief. Harmless, except for the one time they had taken a coach's car for a joyride down High Street with a massive plush Lumberjack strapped to the hood.

But mostly harmless.

She was almost positive that the proof of their antics had been removed from any social media, if not from their possession, and only existed in memory and in retelling when they all got together.

Why should they have grown up simply because they had aged and moved into professional realms?

"I'm afraid to look it up," she admitted with a laugh. "They're probably even more creative now than they were then, and they actually have money . . ." She made a face and looked towards the dugout again. "Sawyer alone would be trouble."

"Seriously?" Jess sat forward, straining in her attempt to see Sawyer in the dugout. "I wouldn't peg Sawyer as a prankster."

Erica applauded as Papa Jim managed to hit a double that sent two of his teammates scoring, then she folded her arms. "The first time I met Sawyer," Erica murmured, leaning closer to her friend and lowering her voice, "he was wearing football pads and a torn-up Belltown practice jersey, swinging a bat at pitches from Cole Hunter, and wearing Grizz's catcher's mask."

Jess stared at her, eyes wide. "What in the world was that supposed to do for him? I've never heard of training like that."

"He wasn't training," Erica laughed, adjusting the wide neck of her T-shirt. "That was after practice. The Six Pack decided that their worst hitter needed more of a challenge, and Sawyer bet them all individual large pizzas that he wouldn't be any worse."

The memory still made Erica giggle, and Jess laughed along with her. "Any worse?" Jess repeated. "Why not be better than he usually was or hit a double or something?"

Now Erica sighed, shaking her head to herself and looking up at the bright-blue sky as she thought back. "He knew better. Cole is no pitcher, but he throws a mean ball, and, knowing his friends, he figured Cole and Grizz had a plan."

"Did they?" Jess asked.

"Of course," Erica replied with a snort. "Cole had picked up a decent cutter without telling him, and Grizz had been practicing with him for weeks."

Jess covered her face, shaking her head as she laughed. "Oh my gosh. So . . .? Did he have to pay out?"

Erica nodded once, sitting forward as the Black Racers took the field again, Sawyer returning to left field, laughing with Creasy as he did so. "Sure did. Turns out football pads are terrible for batting practice and Cole's cutter was way better than anyone expected."

Jess clapped and reached into her popcorn bin for the remaining few kernels. "And why were you there? What were you doing?"

"I had been assigned by the university to be a tutor for the athletic department." She grinned and shrugged. "And the athletic department sent me to baseball."

"Lucky you," Jess told her with a nudge, her mouth curving into a smile.

Erica nodded her agreement, smiling to herself as the game continued and as she watched Sawyer.

Lucky her.

Lucky then, and lucky now.

She bit her lip, a jolt of excitement hitting her gut as she considered that. She'd never thought that she and Sawyer would get back together, that they would have another chance, let alone that she would feel the same way about him as she had before.

That she would feel even more.

That she *could* feel more.

But here she was, and there he was.

And suddenly she was positive he could see her, even from where he was, and he tipped the brim of his cap just enough.

Erica grinned, and she felt that grin light up her heart.

Lucky her indeed.

"Oh, come on, you don't need me here for that."

"Of course I do! Rachel will have told Mom by now, and if I FaceTime without you, I'll get the Spanish Inquisition on my tail."

Erica raised a brow at him as she came back from the kitchen, water in hand, and sank down beside him on his couch, curling her legs up. "I see one of your history courses really sank in."

Sawyer gave her a mocking laugh. "Very funny. I know some things, you know."

"I should hope so." She widened her eyes meaningfully. "I'd have to consider myself a terrible tutor if you didn't."

He shook his head and clamped a hand on her thigh with a faint slap that made her gasp, his fingers gripping tightly and making her giggle.

"Don't do that!" she pleaded, trying to pry his hand away as she laughed. "Please, Sawyer, I can't . . ."

"So this is all about you, huh?" he demanded, intentionally twitching his fingers against her to make the tickling worse.

"No!" she squealed, falling into him, her water sloshing hard against the glass. "No, I take it back!"

He took the water out of her hand and set it safely aside, then used his other hand to drum his fingers against her ribs. "Do you? I think you meant it. I think you actually meant it, Erica."

"Stop!" she cried as tears of mirth leaked from her eyes. "I'm begging you, babe, stop!"

Sawyer did pause, not because she asked, but out of sheer reaction to her endearment.

Babe?

He could get used to that.

Erica sighed in relief, slumping against him and the couch, her cheeks rosy and bright, her dark hair the slightest bit messy in her ponytail.

He wasn't sure she'd ever been more beautiful to him.

"Ugh," she groaned, shaking her head against his shoulder. "I hate when you do that."

He grunted softly in satisfaction. "I haven't done it in a very long time."

She raised her head and rested her chin on his arm. "I know." Her blue eyes seemed to dance with unshed giggles, and he gave in to impulse, leaning down to kiss her.

She arched into it, linking her arms around his neck and pulling herself more upright, her lips eagerly moving with his. Sawyer twisted more fully towards her, sliding one arm around her waist while the other slid between her shoulder blades and into her hair. His fingers slid against her scalp, and she practically purred into the kiss, making him smile against her lips.

Erica had always loved that, and it had been one of his favorite things to do. Her kiss turned tender, though her hold on him tightened, and he took his time in kissing her back, paying respect to every part of her mouth with due diligence. It stunned him how familiar this all was, and how right.

It was as if no time had passed, and yet as if an eternity had.

He'd missed this.

He'd missed *her.*

He broke the kiss gently, then gave her a quick encore peck for good measure.

"I forgot how much I like kissing you," Erica whispered as she nuzzled against him.

Well, if she wanted him to ever do anything else, that wasn't exactly a great way to start.

"Likewise," he assured her, scratching his fingers faintly in her scalp again.

Erica craned her neck with another sigh. "Are you trying to put me to sleep, Sawyer? It's working . . ."

He laughed and yanked his hand out at once, smirking at how much more disheveled her ponytail now was.

It was cute, actually.

"Nope!" he insisted, turning back and reaching for his phone and her water. "Time for the call."

"What? No!" Erica's hands went to her cheeks, then her hair, then back again. "I have Fresh Makeout Face! You can't do that!"

He looked at her in disbelief. "Fresh what? You look fine. Thoroughly kissed, but fine."

"Sawyer!"

She tried to dart from the couch, but he pulled her back, fastening her to his side and giving her a scolding look. "Erica. You're beautiful just like this. And my mom won't care if you look like I kissed you or not. I might get a better Christmas present if she does think I kissed you, okay?"

Erica looked skeptical suddenly. "So this is all about you, huh?"

He heaved a sigh and dropped an arm over her shoulder. "I'll break out the cookies if you stay."

She didn't even think about it. "Deal," she said, pressing the screen of his phone and expertly bringing up his mom's number on FaceTime and starting the call.

"Huh," he grunted. "Do you want to talk to my mom by yourself, and I'll just go clean the bathroom or something?"

Erica nudged him hard. "I saw your bathroom, and you can't call that cleaning. I'll do it when we're done."

"You're not cleaning my bathroom, Erica," he insisted.

"Who's doing what?" chirped a familiar voice from his phone.

They both looked down at the screen and saw not just his mom's face, but that of Todd Landers, his arm draped around Sawyer's mom just like Sawyer's was around Erica.

Nobody said anything for a moment as they all looked at each other.

"Hi Erica," Sawyer's mom said with a forced yet still sincere smile.

Erica waved weakly. "Hi, Sally. Hi, Mr. Landers."

Todd nodded, his smile possibly the worst of the group. "Hey, Erica. Sawyer."

"Todd," Sawyer greeted, though he probably should have

gone for the respectful address Erica had instead of a simple first name.

He cleared his throat. "And hi, Mom."

His mom's smile warmed a little. "Hi, sweetie."

There was another long pause.

"Well, this is awkward, isn't it?" Todd finally said with a chuckle.

Sawyer took a good look at the guy, button-up shirt, no tie, graying hair, crisp glasses, and all. He looked almost exactly like he remembered from the Belltown days, affectionate position with Sawyer's mom aside.

Strange how that changed things.

But, also strangely, Sawyer wasn't exactly upset.

Erica put a hand on his knee, rubbing very gently, and he smiled at the sensation, pulling her a little closer to him. "Eh, I've had worse," he commented, answering Todd's question. "Rachel made me stand in as a dance partner when she was preparing for an audition back in high school, remember that, Mom?"

He could see the relief in his mother's eyes and expression, and the increased pressure of Erica's hand mirrored it.

He'd meant what he said when he first found out about Todd. He wasn't upset about it, and he didn't object to the guy in particular at all.

He'd just wanted to know about it.

But in spite of all that, he would do what he could to make this smooth.

Or, at least, less awkward.

The conversation quickly turned to their game that day, and Todd surprised Sawyer with how much he knew about the Black Racer players and their stats. Only when Erica and his mom begged them for a change in topic did they switch off to Erica's museum and her assignment in Arizona. Sawyer had to smile, hearing Erica talk about the Kids Day and the field trips she got to deal with, which she clearly enjoyed more than the museum assignment itself.

She really needed to be teaching full-time with passion like that, and her adjunct position wasn't giving her enough.

It was helping, she told him often, but she wanted more.

Todd looked at Sawyer's mom, then said, "Well, I'm going to find something to do, and I think I heard Erica say something about cleaning a bathroom?"

Erica nodded at once. "Yep. Trust me, it needs it."

"Hey!" Sawyer protested. "And I told you not to clean it. Come on, you did not come over to clean."

"Too late!" she chirped, giving him a quick kiss on his cheek before pushing off of the couch. "Bye, Sal! Bye, Todd!"

Todd waved and moved out of the screen while Erica practically skipped away.

Sawyer stared after her, then looked at his mom. "Apparently we need to talk."

His mom chuckled and settled into the couch. "So it seems."

Neither of them said anything for a moment, and then his mother sighed. "Why didn't you tell me you'd reconnected with Erica, sweetheart?"

Sawyer smiled at her as gently as he could. "Why didn't you tell me about Todd?" he returned, keeping his tone kind and warm.

He wasn't angry in any way, and he needed her to know that.

Confused, but not angry.

"I don't know," his mom admitted, rubbing at her neck. "I wasn't . . . I didn't . . . Are you upset, Sawyer?"

He shook his head. "No, Mom, I'm not. I want you to be happy. If you're happy with Todd, that's all I want. He seems great, and his daughters are awesome, I remember. I just wish you'd told me."

She smiled in apology. "Oh, sweetie. Todd and I took things so slowly. We weren't even sure it was going to work or that there was anything there. It was a very gradual, natural thing. I didn't have anything really to tell until a few months ago, and then . . ." She shrugged, and her eyes grew teary. "I didn't know how you and Rachel would feel. You both miss your dad so terribly, and I think about him every day. I was afraid, and I'm sorry."

Sawyer sat up, exhaling audibly. "Rachel and I talked, Mom. We don't feel like you're replacing Dad, and we don't think Dad would want you to be alone forever. You don't need to be sorry. Does Todd make you happy?"

The change in her smile alone gave him the answer. She looked away, probably at Todd if her smile were any indication. "Yeah. Yeah, he does. And he makes me laugh. And he actually likes doing the dishes."

"Wow." Sawyer whistled, shaking his head. "Tell me he likes landscaping and I'll send him a fruit basket."

His mom laughed and looked back at him. "He *loves* landscaping."

"Okay, I'll make the call as soon as we're done. Deluxe fruit basket coming up."

She laughed again. "Oh, honey. I love you, you know that?"

"I've heard," he replied with a wink. "Love you too, Mom. I'll call you after we play Cole next week, okay?"

"Sounds good, Skeeter. And you're going to tell me about Erica then, deal?"

He barked a laugh. "Deal. Bye, Mom." He pressed End Call, smiled, and tossed the phone onto the couch.

The faucet in the bathroom suddenly switched on, and

he pushed himself off of the couch. "Erica Anne, I meant it when I said don't clean that bathroom!"

"Too late!" she bellowed. "How about you start working on that paper you need to turn in to me?"

"We said school was off limits, woman! And maybe I've already started."

"And maybe I'm Babe Ruth. Make yourself useful and start on the toilet." She tossed a rag at him.

He raised a brow. "Do I get credit for helping my teacher clean a bathroom?"

Erica stopped and gave him an exasperated look. "If you can turn cleaning your own bathroom into some sort of legitimate cultural experience worthy of a three-page paper, I'll give you an assignment credit, okay?"

Sawyer grinned in victory, though he had no idea how he was going to manage it. "Okay, Teach. Watch and learn."

# CHAPTER 9

"HAVE I EVER told you that I actually hate parties?"

"Once or twice, yeah. And you may have mentioned it on the drive over."

"I was trying to drop a hint!"

Sawyer chuckled, nudging Erica as she stood almost awkwardly close to him instead of mingling with the other players and their families. Or significant others, as the case might be. "Yeah. I tripped over the hint."

Erica glared at him, nudging back a little too hard. "So why are we here?"

He leaned over, his mouth brushing her ear. "Because these are my teammates and my friends. And you're one of us now, sweetheart."

A flash of her wrist landed a perfect smack against his chest, and he chuckled with a hint of a wheeze, rubbing the area tenderly.

"Knock it off," she hissed, her cheeks flaming even as she smiled. "I may be your girlfriend, but it hasn't been long enough for me to officially join this club. I'm here to support you, babe, but I'd much rather be at home in sweats, watching a movie with popcorn."

Sawyer nodded, suddenly feeling much the same way. "Sounds great. Let's make the rounds so we can get to that."

Erica looked up at him in confusion. "I didn't bring sweats with me, Skeet."

He matched her look with his own. "I have sweats at the apartment. I don't know if you knew this, but I really like sweats. And I tend to get a lot of them in my profession, so, conveniently, I have quite the collection."

His girlfriend raised a brow, as she usually did when he teased her. "You may never get them back. I'm a bit of a hoarder with comfy clothing."

"I'll survive."

They shared a smile, and she slipped an arm around his waist. "Sometimes I really like you, Sawyer Bennett."

He leaned down again, this time to kiss her softly. "Sometimes I really like you too."

"Aww, you're the cutest couple I've ever seen."

Sawyer rolled his eyes and turned to glare at Mace. "Really? With how you and Jess were after your wedding?"

Mace shrugged, grinning without shame in his golf polo. "Have to make it look good, Skeeter. I have a reputation to uphold."

"Oh, do you want us to tamp this down?" Erica offered helpfully, gesturing between herself and Sawyer. "I wouldn't want to start a competition here, if you've got a reputation."

Sawyer snorted, then turned it into a fake cough, sipping his soda to cover it.

Mace ignored him and adopted a fond look as he considered Erica. "I like you." He looked at Sawyer, jerking his thumb towards Erica. "I like her. Keep her, would you?" He winked at Erica and strolled away, calling out to Papa Jim about the number of ribs he was eating.

Keep her? Why wouldn't he keep her?

Sawyer swallowed, his eyes widening.

Oh. KEEP her.

Keep.

He'd love to, quite honestly. This was so easy, so comfortable, and Erica understood him. She knew him, knew what he needed, and complemented him so perfectly.

So why hadn't he told her everything yet?

His mind flashed back to dinner with Ryker and Grizz, and the back of his neck began to heat with guilt.

She needed to know. If he really wanted to keep her, wanted to tell her how he *really* felt . . .

He glanced around the house, filled with people inside and out, trying to find some place for privacy that didn't involve a bedroom, bathroom, or pantry. Finally, he just took Erica's hand and murmured, "Come with me?"

She nodded without question and let him lead her from the house, and the two of them just walked silently side by side down the street as the sun set over the Arizona horizon.

"Where are we going?" Erica asked, not sounding as though she particularly minded what his answer was.

Sawyer smiled at her, squeezing her hand. "You'll see."

The more he thought about it, the more he liked his current destination though. They'd passed it as they drove into Hanks's neighborhood, and Erica had even commented on how fun it was. He hoped it would still be a fun place when all of this was over.

Soon enough, they were there, and Erica laughed softly. "The playground? Really?"

Sawyer nodded, smiling as much as he dared. "Come on. Get on the swing. I'll push you."

Erica did so, shaking her head as she still laughed. "I haven't done this in years," she commented as he pushed her gently.

"Me neither." He swallowed with difficulty, his throat suddenly tight. "Erica, I need to tell you some things."

She glanced over her shoulder. "I figured as much. Come around so I can see you, please."

That was fair. He moved around the swing beside her and came to lean against the pole nearby, looking down at the ground.

"Sawyer . . ."

He looked at her, swinging just the smallest bit now, smiling at him. "What?"

She nodded once. "Go ahead. I'm listening."

His attention returned to the ground, and he exhaled slowly once more. "I told you that I threw myself into baseball after my dad died, that I basically gave up my education and did everything I could to improve myself there."

He saw her nod again, but it barely registered.

"I didn't tell you that I felt pressure to provide for my mom and my sister, just like my dad had," he admitted, his voice dipping with a strained emotion he hadn't anticipated. "And the only way I could do that quickly was to get drafted. I had to cut out everything else in my life to make sure that I didn't let my dad down, that I could take care of our family without him. He had never missed one of my games, had always believed I could be a better player than I thought I was, and suddenly he wasn't there to tell me those things. To motivate me or advise me."

Sawyer cleared his throat, fighting against the burning sensation there. This was all so much harder than he'd planned, but he couldn't stop. Everything he had felt back then suddenly rose to the surface, ready to come spilling out of him with a recklessness that frightened him. "So I had to do it on my own. Baseball became my life and my business. I ignored absolutely everything else in my life except for baseball."

He hesitated and shook his head with a wince. "Well, and my family. Rachel started hating me for trying to turn into her father. That didn't last long, but I didn't know what else to do. I didn't know my dad had set things up nicely so that Mom and Rach would be okay, let alone that I would, and since I never told Mom what I was doing . . ."

The swing creaked softly as Erica continued to gently sway in it, but he barely heard her.

"College wasn't fun anymore; you were right," he admitted, his throat feeling raw. "It was a means to an end. I had a scholarship, so I took whatever classes would help my baseball career. Baseball wasn't fun anymore; it was my ticket to becoming who I thought my father needed me to be. The man who could take care of the family, even if they didn't need me to."

He'd never told anyone all of this, and honestly, he wasn't sure he'd ever really put it together in his mind for himself. But here with Erica, he could lay the pieces side by side and attempt to make sense of it, explain it, and maybe, just maybe, get over it.

He turned slightly, sliding a hand into his pocket. "I don't think I really enjoyed baseball again until after I was drafted. I had a contract with Orlando, and I felt secure. Then suddenly it was fun again. I felt free from the burdens of pressure and expectation. I had a great rookie season, made some waves, and ensured I wouldn't get dropped unless I really screwed up. Since I don't screw up, I would be fine."

"Sure," Erica murmured, still swinging a little. "You've always been very careful that way."

Sawyer nodded and looked back at Erica, meeting her eyes steadily. "After that rookie season, I was feeling pretty good about myself. Until I remembered what I promised my dad before he died."

The swinging stopped. "What?"

"I promised that I would finish my degree," Sawyer told her, his voice suddenly going hoarse. This was the part, strangely enough, that he was most afraid to confess to her, of all people.

He straightened a little. "No one knows that, not my mother, not the Six Pack. Everybody knows I didn't graduate, but no one knows why, and no one knows why I'm taking classes now. You and Mace are the only ones who even know about the classes at all."

Sawyer managed a weak smile, and she returned it at once, instantly encouraging him to share more. "I decided to start taking the online courses, slowly working my way towards the degree again. But I'm not driven to finish. I should be, but I'm not. So long as I am taking classes, any classes, I'm working on my promise to Dad. The day that I finish, the promise will be fulfilled. And then I won't have anything to prove. Anything to drive me. Any connection to Dad."

He lowered his eyes again, his eyes burning, to his surprise. "And then what? I keep playing baseball. I keep improving, making money, living my dream."

He snorted softly, a newfound bitterness seeping into this strange confession of his. "Living the dream. Does anybody know how hard it is to live your dream? The risk of failure is so much worse, and the pressure of it all is incredible. It doesn't even feel like the dream sometimes, just my job. I love it; I will always love it, but . . ."

He shifted his attention to the sky, now streaked with colors of sunset. "It wasn't my only dream. Leaving Belltown without you felt like a defeat I'd never recover from. I knew I had to, or thought I knew, but going into this dream life felt strange without you, once I looked up enough to realize I didn't have a life anymore. And now you're back, and I . . ."

He leaned his head back against the pole and met her eyes once more, feeling stripped bare and raw for her examination. "I couldn't let this go any further without making sure you knew everything. About the past, about our breakup, about my classes . . . even about baseball. You mean enough to me to know it all."

Erica stared back at him, her expression unreadable, her blue eyes filled with a light he couldn't decipher. Her hands were clasped and resting on her thighs, her hair slung over one shoulder, one foot twisting very slightly in the dirt beneath it.

And she said nothing.

Slowly she inhaled, and he tensed, waiting.

"I love you."

He blinked at her. What did she say?

Her perfect lips curved into a gentle, tender smile. "I love you, Sawyer. I knew it before you told me this, but now . . . I really, really love you." She shook her head, blinking quickly, a hand going to her chest. "I can't even . . ."

He didn't let her finish, moving to her and taking her face in his hands, kissing her with all the relief, passion, and exhilaration currently coursing into every ounce of his being. He kissed her like there was no tomorrow, as if his life depended on it, as though she were everything.

Because she was.

Breathing was unnecessary, thinking was irrelevant, and existing was only through this connection. Only with Erica.

Only now.

She gripped the back of his neck in a vice, giving as good as he gave, and he wondered, briefly, if death could come from an implosion of too much emotion, too much sensation, or too much ridiculous good fortune.

"I love you too, baby," he whispered, nipping gently at her lips. "So much."

Erica sighed, rubbing her fingers against the back of his neck, then pulling him close for the tightest hug he could ever remember receiving.

And for the first time in several years, he felt whole.

He buried his face into Erica's shoulder, gripping her hair, and reveled in the feeling.

Whole. With her.

Oh, yes, he was keeping her.

He was keeping this.

Sawyer hung over the dugout fence, warmup on, chatting with Adam, neither of them pitching today.

Erica could have watched him be this relaxed forever.

He was all smiles, laughing and teasing his teammates as they warmed up. She had no idea what he was saying, of course, and barely knew his teammates enough to even try to guess what they could be teased about. She knew the girl-friends and wives more than the players themselves, Mace aside, though she could honestly say she could identify the regular starters by name without help.

She laughed as she watched Adam and Sawyer attempt to spit sunflower shells at Mace as he walked by, earning them both vows of eternal punishment, or whatever threats Mace liked to toss out. Adam and Sawyer didn't seem to be particularly concerned about whatever it was.

Those two . . .

Adam and Sawyer were about the same age, though Adam was from Montreal and had played ball at Stanford. The boys called him Indy, probably because his last name was Jones, and he'd taken to mimicking the motion of a whip at the end of a good inning. Sawyer had told her the guy even had the worn-looking leather jacket befitting the character, though he hadn't brought it to Arizona, for obvious reasons.

Adam was just as mischievous as any of the Six Pack had ever been, and she wouldn't be surprised if he got adopted as a bonus member one of these days. He was on the fast track to being considered for the All-Star team, so who knew what that would do for his association with the rest.

Once they were back in Ohio, she wondered what kind of antics Sawyer, Adam, and Mace would get up to together.

There was just no telling.

"Hi, Erica!" Hannah Jones greeted, waving excitedly as she came into the row to sit by her, bright-blond hair almost glowing in the light of day. The girl was tall, tanned, and trim, which made Erica a little sick, but she was also, hands down, the nicest woman Erica had ever met.

One of those women you want to hate but can't hate, and you're conflicted the entire time by their maddening perfection.

Apparently she was also a domestic goddess and a computer scientist, and she spoke French fluently.

Erica really, really wanted to hate her.

Did that make her a terrible person?

She shook off her thoughts and grinned, standing to give her a quick hug. "Hi, Hannah. Where's Abby?"

Hannah grinned at the mention of her daughter, but waved a hand in the air before adjusting her Black Racer tank-top strap. "Oh, I'm letting her have a day with Grandma today. She was so excited, I just *had* to sacrifice bringing my two-year-old diva child to her daddy's baseball game on a hot Arizona afternoon." She widened her eyes and dropped down into her seat, crossing her long, exposed legs and dropping them into the row below them. "My gosh, can someone get me an adult beverage while I've got the chance to have one?"

Erica threw her head back and laughed. "I don't have any of those, but I did manage to sneak chocolate in."

"I love you," Hannah gushed, holding her hand out. "You are my new best friend."

"Oh good."

They were soon joined by Jess, and the three of them laughed and chatted while they waited for the game to start.

"Did I hear that you're an adjunct professor?" Hannah asked her as she tossed a candy into her mouth. "What does that even mean?"

Erica shrugged a shoulder. "Means I teach classes without being an official employee of the university, more or less. I don't have a teaching degree, technically, though I did do an education minor."

Jess frowned slightly. "I thought you worked for a museum."

"I do," she assured her. "History major, education minor. Almost a humanities minor too."

"Overachiever," Hannah muttered with a nudge.

Erica laughed. "Indecisive, more like. I did a lot of tutoring in college, which is how I met Sawyer and his gang. I tutored them for a bit."

"Ahh," Hannah said with a nod. "And Sawyer was hot for teacher?"

Her cheeks flamed at once. "Oh, stop!"

Jess flashed a quick smile. "Tell the truth, Erica . . ."

Erica bit her lip, her cheeks absolutely burning now. "He might have been," she whispered.

The girls squealed, clapping like kids, and Erica covered her face with a groan. "Oh my gosh . . ."

"Back to your job," Hannah said quickly. "So your museum lets you teach too?"

Erica nodded, dropping her hands and hoping her face

would cool soon. "As long as it doesn't affect my work there, they don't care. The supplemental income from Belltown is nice. Not enough to live on, obviously, but nice. I'm hoping that if I do well enough, it'll look good enough on a resume to get me a real teaching gig in the future."

Jess shook her head, munching on popcorn as she usually did at games. "Two jobs, multiple areas of study, farmgirl, tutor, and a hunky pitcher boyfriend. Hannah's right. You're an overachiever."

"Guilty as charged," Erica quipped, reaching for popcorn, then combining it with some chocolate as she tossed it into her mouth. "Oh well."

They rose quickly for the national anthem, as did all the other fans, then stayed standing to cheer appropriately for the visiting team, their voices and applause much more exuberant when the Black Racers were announced.

Erica and the others sat as the Black Racers took the field. "Who's pitching today?" she asked.

"Hanksy, I think." Hannah squinted, then nodded. "Yep, that's him."

Right as she confirmed it, the announcer named the starting lineup, and she threw up her hands, shaking her head, making the others laugh.

Erica eyed the first batter, trying to size him up. "He looks intense . . ."

Jess nodded, still munching her popcorn. "Yep. He was at the Home Run Derby two years ago. Didn't make it last year, has a bit of a chip on his shoulder about it."

"How do you know that?" Hannah demanded.

"My husband," Jess replied with a smug little dance in her chair. "He's secretly a gossipmonger."

"No," Erica gasped in mock surprise before rolling her eyes. It was the most obvious thing in the world. Mace knew everyone and everything; he had impeccable instincts for sniffing things out and an insatiable curiosity. He was the go-to guy if you wanted information on anyone in the majors.

He was dangerous that way.

She wondered just what he knew about the Six Pack.

And what she could tell him.

She smiled to herself, glancing back over to Sawyer and Adam, now wearing their hats inside out and backwards, still on the fence, now shouting encouragements to their team-mates.

What dorks.

Adorable dorks, but still.

Hanks struck out the first two batters, prompting Sawyer and Adam to pound the fence rails in enthusiasm.

Erica nudged Hannah. "Think they're excited?"

Hannah looked, then sighed in despair. "I swear he's an adult. He is."

Jess hummed to herself, ignoring the dugout completely. "Do you ever really look at your man in baseball pants and just want to say thank you?"

"What?" Erica laughed, looking at the redhead in shock.

She shrugged, chomping on more popcorn. "Serious. That's my man down there, and he is just so nice even from this angle. Every time the ump moves away from him, it's just . . . Mmm." She shook her head and pretended to shiver. "Money."

Hannah and Erica shared a bewildered look. "I guess . . ." Erica said slowly.

"Give me a tailored suit over a baseball uniform any day," Hannah huffed with a crooked smirk. "That'll get me shivering."

The crowd suddenly gasped, and all three women sat up, too caught up in the conversation to have seen what happened.

Hanks lay on the mound, gripping his right elbow, teeth clenched.

"Oh no," Erica breathed, looking up at the jumbotron for a replay.

Hanks had pitched the ball as usual, but his arm had snapped into a strange sidearm throw, his forearm almost going slack and the ball going wide.

Erica hissed and looked back out on the field where Sarge, Damien—who coached the pitchers—Mace, and a gray-haired man in a polo now crowded around Hanks.

"Where's Jamie?" Hannah asked at once, looking around and getting out of her seat. "She's going to be a mess."

"Who's with Sarge and Mace?" Erica whispered to Jess.

"Doc," she replied. "He's the head athletic trainer." Her expression was tense, and her hands clenched.

Erica looked over at the dugout, where Sawyer and Adam had leaped the fence, their hats off, staring at their fellow pitcher in horror.

Now what happened?

She looked back to the mound, where they were able to sit Hanks up, then help him to his feet and awkwardly walk him off the field.

Damien jogged over to Sawyer, put his hand on his arm, and Erica saw Sawyer stiffen, swallow, and nod. Then he shucked his warmup, giving it to Adam, grabbed his cap and mitt, and jogged out to the mound.

"What's happening?" Erica demanded. "Sawyer doesn't pitch until tomorrow!"

Jess shook her head, her mouth gaping slightly. "This almost never happens. It's too early in the game for a reliever, I guess. Mace says they don't have a good long reliever yet, so they're moving up the rotation so they don't burn through multiple relievers. Oh man." She glanced at Erica, then turned to her more fully. "It's going to be fine. Sawyer's great under pressure, and we shouldn't have any trouble with this team. It's fine."

Erica swallowed and nodded as she watched Sawyer and Mace chat on the mound, then as Mace jogged back behind home plate and caught a few warmup pitches from Sawyer.

Sawyer didn't look fine.

He didn't look fine at all.

# CHAPTER 10

"WELL, IT WAS a bit of a shocking loss for the Black Racers in preseason games today down in the Cactus League. They went down five to one to the Kansas City Hawks, and really, this game was over before it ever reached the third inning, Brett."

"Sure was, Kyle. Look at this, Nate Hanks, arguably their best pitcher, third batter of the game. Of the game, Kyle. We're still in the top of the first here!"

"And it's an ugly one. You can see him release that ball early, goes wide for a wild pitch, Mason Benjamin catches, and down goes Hanks. He just grabs that right elbow, and you knew he was done for the night, and could be the rest of the season."

"They're calling it an olecranon fracture, Kyle, but with a pitcher, you've gotta wonder about those ligaments. No one is saying Tommy John surgery yet, but you gotta wonder."

"The game could have been saved, manager Mark Palmer making the bold move of not going with a reliever. Instead he pulled starting pitcher Sawyer Bennett, a Six Pack guy. Brett, can you explain what happened here?"

"I can't, Kyle. I just can't. He started off okay, but he was just not in his groove tonight."

"None of them were. Errors in the outfield and slow responses . . . Not a good night for the Racers, Brett. Mark Palmer has gotta be scratching his head today. We might see some interesting lineup changes for today's game against Baltimore."

Sawyer switched off the TV, tossing the remote onto the cushion beside him, though he continued to stare at the screen as if it were still on.

He couldn't explain what had happened last night. Nothing had been wrong, his arm had felt good, and he'd closed out the first inning without a problem. They'd warmed him up a bit more during the bottom of the first while his team batted, and going into the second, he'd thought he could keep up Hanksy's great start.

But things had fallen apart.

The infield had had their work cut out for them, and they'd kept his mistakes from getting too out of hand. But that hadn't lasted the whole game, and by the seventh, it was like they had never played together before.

They'd all been shaken up by seeing Hanksy go down, and every pitcher in the world feared that exact scenario, but there was no excuse for completely abandoning their skills and practice to a team they should have easily beaten.

Sarge had pulled Sawyer from the game in the seventh, when it became apparent that he was useless on the mound, and Cavins had closed them out easily and with quick efficiency. He'd ensured his position on the team with that showing, and Sawyer was proud of him.

It shouldn't have been necessary, but he would give credit where credit was due.

Sawyer would have given anything to not face his team today, to not show up for the game and to avoid sitting in the dugout with them. He was supposed to be a team leader, a captain without officially being a captain. The pitcher set the tone for the entire team, and the tone he had set had been a miserable one.

He hadn't talked to a single person after the game. He'd have gone straight to the locker room after he had been pulled if he didn't think that would be splashed all across the sports pages and broadcasts. He wasn't a player with a temper or foul attitude, and he wasn't going to become one now.

It had been torture to sit there and watch the team play below their potential, knowing he had led them there.

Erica had tried to make him feel better, but nothing had helped. She didn't understand. He needed to do something, not just get over it or move on.

Bad games happened, and he was no stranger to them.

This hadn't been just a bad game.

This had been a horrible game.

Miserable.

The sort of game that made people question.

Sawyer more than anyone.

They played Baltimore today. Rabbit's team.

They'd been excited about playing against each other and seeing if Ryker could get a piece of one of Sawyer's pitches.

Now he would be trying to get a piece of Indy's.

Didn't do anything for the Six Pack rivalry. The media would be disappointed.

Not that he cared.

Win or lose, one of them would be buying dinner for the other, and that was it. No bets today, just a meal.

Sawyer wished he were pitching tonight. He could redeem himself for yesterday. He could prove himself better—the pitcher everybody expected and wanted him to be.

Not the loser from last night.

His phone buzzed, and he pulled it from the pocket of his hoodie, glancing at the screen.

It was from Erica.

*Hey, babe. Hope you slept well. Love you.*

He swallowed. He'd probably hurt her last night, being a bit short and letting his frustration get the better of him. But she was a tough girl, and she'd held his hand the entire drive home, softly stroking her thumb against his hand.

That had been the only comforting thing he'd had all night.

No comforting words, no pats to the back, no encouragement, just that.

Just her skin brushing against his.

It hadn't made everything better, but it had taken the edge off.

He knew better than to alienate himself from her or from anyone else. He was better than that now, and wiser too. He knew he needed her.

He didn't know what to do, or how she could help, but he needed her.

He exhaled and typed out a quick *Love you too*, and he leaned his head back against the couch after sending it.

The phone buzzed again, and he furrowed his brow, hoping Erica wasn't trying to have a conversation about feelings this early in the morning. It would be a very short conversation, and she wouldn't get much out of it.

He looked at the phone, then raised his head.

Six Pack group text.

Cole had kicked it off. *Anybody see Grizz dive into the stands last night? So graceful.*

Sawyer actually managed a smile at that. No, he hadn't seen it. He'd been so concerned with his own game that he hadn't even paid attention to how anyone else had done.

Levi was the first to respond. *All those dance classes he took really paid off, huh? Pointed toes and all.*

Axel posted three quick GIFs of spectacular falls, then replied, *I give it a 5. His takeoff was horrible.*

Ryker reacted to the GIFs with laughing emojis before saying, *AND he knocked over that kid's nachos.*

Sawyer laughed now and typed, *Not the nachos! Grizzy, did you pay for more?*

*Whatever, you guys,* Grizz replied. *Perfect swan dive, and I got the redhead's number for you, Steal.*

Sawyer had no idea what he was talking about, but he wasn't going to switch the TV back on to find out. He didn't want to see any more sports highlights right now, especially since he was destined to hear more about himself before he saw anything amusing about Grizz.

He could play along with the reactions, though, and act as though he were fully caught up.

They'd never know, and they wouldn't talk about his night. Unspoken rule of the Six Pack: never talk about bad games. Losses were okay, but any really bad nights were never brought up.

Levi sent three thumbs up, then added, *But what about the nachos???*

The rest were all quick to agree with that before Grizz replied, *I gave the kid the ball and we took a selfie. He's fine.*

Cole fired back at once. *Grizz selfies pay for nachos now? Shoot, I'll be eating nachos for weeks.*

Axel jumped into the fray with, *Game balls are going as currency? Can I get a soft pretzel, please?*

Sawyer threw in a couple of jabs about working on grace, coordination, and core strength to improve proper stands-diving form, and Ryker brought up the more crucial point of asking if Grizz actually caught the ball.

*Yes, you scwewy Wabbit, I did,* he replied, attaching a GIF of Elmer Fudd with a rifle.

Never to be outdone, Ryker replied with a GIF of Bugs Bunny running circles around a very confused Elmer Fudd.

Sawyer shook his head. This was going to get ugly.

*Looks like it's Rabbit season, boys,* Grizz replied. *Tell your guys to hold nothing back tonight, Skeeter.*

No one said anything for a bit, and Sawyer wondered if they were feeling as uncomfortable as Sawyer himself was about the statement.

Probably not, but it might still strike them as awkward all the same.

There was no way they were as uncomfortable as he was. They couldn't be.

Sawyer replied quickly, just a brief *You got it,* and then he dropped the phone on the couch, pushing off of the couch himself and moving towards the bedroom to change. He was going to the park early to get some film time in, toss a few pitches just to loosen up, check in with Doc and Kayla about starting preventative rehab for his arm, and, if there was still time before the team left for the game, get some studying for History of Sport in.

He'd been neglecting his coursework lately, which couldn't have been a surprise given his schedule as well as his dating life with Erica, but Hanksy's injury gave him pause.

Injuries could happen to a pitcher at any time. The strain on their shoulders and arms was incredible, and even someone who had no history of issues could suddenly develop some—and potentially serious issues at that. Season-ending issues.

Career-ending issues.

And then he would be really stuck.

This was why his dad had wanted him to get his degree, but Sawyer hadn't listened.

He had to finish as soon as possible. He needed a backup for his life if disaster struck.

And he needed to focus, practice, and prepare to avoid needing that backup at all.

He needed to do it all now.

It was one of the most uncomfortable baseball games she had ever sat through in her entire life.

Sawyer hadn't even been playing, and she felt that.

Someone who didn't know him would have thought Sawyer Bennett simply very focused on the game, watching from the dugout and standing at the fence there.

She wouldn't deny that he was exactly that; she also knew it wasn't just focus.

He was completely engrossed. He watched every move Adam made on the mound, every twitch a batter made, every ball he pitched, and every replay as though he'd be tested on it later. And he paid just as much attention to the visiting team.

When his teammates returned to the dugout for batting, he barely spoke to any of them. Adam and Mace were able to get some conversation out of him, but that was it. When Jesse was put in as reliever in the sixth inning, Sawyer became even more intent.

Erica couldn't understand why. Sawyer wasn't a reliever, and he'd never been. Jesse was their best reliever, she'd been told, but he was a pitcher for quick efficiency, not endurance.

Adam had had a great game, so she had to guess Sarge was just saving him, since they were winning.

The team looked far better today than they had the last game.

Sawyer clearly noticed too.

His emotions on that fact were less clear. He would absolutely have been proud of his team and happy they were succeeding, but he didn't look proud or pleased. He showed no emotion whatsoever.

No signs of pleasure, no bursts of anger, no expression of victory.

He was just . . . there.

Baltimore was a good team, but the Black Racers really gelled and proved their skills. The media had tried to make a point of the Six Pack; she saw them pull Sawyer from the dugout before the game for a picture with Ryker.

He hadn't smiled.

He and Ryker had chatted just before the game had started, but not extensively, and the only thing she could say about Sawyer was that he had shaken Ryker's hand and patted him on the back.

She wasn't sure how the Six Pack usually greeted each other on the field, but that didn't seem like their usual way.

Something was definitely up, and she knew it was about yesterday's game, but she didn't know more than that. He wasn't talking about it, and she didn't think she ought to push.

No one could blame him for being off yesterday, not after seeing Hanks go down and then having to come in unexpectedly. It had been a risky move for Sarge and one she definitely did not agree with. The whole team had been off after that, and there was nothing Sawyer could do about that. He was not responsible for the entire team and how they played, and he ought to know that.

Erica would have told him all of this if only she had a moment to actually talk to him.

He hadn't said much at all last night, and she hadn't even seen him this morning. He'd said he needed to prep for the game, but they would talk later.

She got that he needed space, and she would give it to him, but she couldn't help being worried.

Jess and Hannah had started off sitting by her again, but once it became clear that Erica wasn't going to be much more talkative than Sawyer was being, they had drifted away to sit with some of the others. She didn't mind, and she knew they wouldn't take offense.

One of the responsibilities of the significant other of a professional athlete was to bear their burdens with them, small or great, and Erica wasn't entirely sure which category this fell into.

Until she knew the extent of it, and how to help, she simply had to bear it.

Which was maddening.

She wanted to do something, say something—anything, really, if it would help him. It had been years since she'd had to deal with a bad game for Sawyer, and she couldn't be sure that what had worked before would work now. He was more mature now, more seasoned, but what impact would that have on things like this?

With all that he had revealed to her the other day—a moving, vulnerable, raw confession—she couldn't be sure. Nothing had ever touched her more than his confiding in her, and she treasured the trust and respect he had shown. She loved him for it, knowing how difficult it must have been to share those things, and how determined he was to appear strong and proud at all times.

But knowing those things gave her more reason for concern and added multiple layers to the possibilities of what was affecting him.

If he didn't tell her, how could she know?

*Time,* she reminded herself. *Give him time.*

Time she could give. Patience she could give.

Love she could give.

If only he would give to her. Insight, for one thing, and a direction he needed her to take.

Despite the depth of it, their relationship was still so new.

The feelings from college had never gone away; they were both well aware of it, and so she could excuse the speed at which they had reached their current state. But with that speed also came the risk of missing so many crucial developments.

She felt like she was missing a few now.

She heaved a sigh of relief as the game ended, applauding with the rest of the crowd and rising from her seat. She glanced over at the dugout again, only to find Sawyer gone.

Strange, he was usually up on the field at the end of the game, high-fiving his teammates as they came in and giving encouraging words, if not joking around.

Something was wrong, and she needed to find out what it was.

*Ryker.* Ryker would be able to draw him out and bring him back to himself. The Six Pack always met up after the games against each other; they would owe dinner one way or the other.

Brightening, Erica tossed her purse over her head and across one shoulder, moving out of the stands and down towards the player locker rooms. It would be a bit before she saw either Sawyer or Ryker, but she refused to risk missing a single moment.

She took up position leaning against a support pillar, eying both the doors to the visiting team's room as well as the clubhouse for the Black Racers. She kept a polite smile on her face as people came and went, mostly stadium crew and other family members. Then she saw some of the Black Racer bullpen come out, all of whom greeted her with wide smiles and nods.

Any time now. Sawyer was usually pretty quick with showering and changing. The only holdup might be last-minute coaching reminders or meetings, but he usually texted her if those were happening.

She checked her phone just in case.

Nothing.

She frowned at the screen, then pocketed it, forcing herself not to think too much of it. Overthinking would get her into the same sort of problems that Sawyer was undoubtedly getting into. She would be in no state to help him if she was also tangled up in knots.

Strange how being in a relationship made one both more comfortable and more insecure at the same time.

She'd never been a fan of that.

Not that she had a reason to be insecure with Sawyer. She absolutely believed that he loved her; she felt it with every look he gave her and every brush of his hand. He was sincere in everything he did with her, and there was a warm familiarity to being with him that she would not get with anyone else. If he ever thought that he was making her insecure or worrying her or giving her any reason to doubt, he would have been mortified and ashamed. He would have moved heaven and earth to prove himself to her.

That was the thing about Sawyer Bennett. He was as intense with everything in his life as he was about baseball. He was hard on himself in every aspect and expected the best of himself at all times, though he was forgiving, generous, and exceptionally patient with other people.

Why he couldn't extend the same mercy to himself that he did to everyone else, she would never know. She loved him, but she wished he would give himself a break.

He deserved one.

The visitors' locker-room door opened, and out strode Ryker Stone, his white-blond hair darkened from the shower, his blue eyes a muted shade in the shadows of the stadium. He looked around, then saw Erica, and he grinned his trademark grin, hefting his duffel onto his shoulder as he moved in her direction.

"Well, well, well," he drawled, "maybe I'm a lucky guy after all."

Erica smiled back, shaking her head. "That line is so old, Ryker."

He shrugged, still grinning. "I prefer the term 'classic,' if you don't mind." He dropped his bag and opened his arms, and she practically ran into them, giggling as he lifted her off the ground. "Oh, it's good to see you, Teach. Seriously, it's been way too long."

She patted his shoulders as he set her down, then took his face in hand as though she were his mother. "Wow, you've gotten old."

"Hey!" he protested, swatting her back lightly.

She rubbed under his chin teasingly. "And this? Come on, Ryker. You look worse than Axel."

"I do not! Axel's is nasty. This is very dashing and scruffy, and it all comes off when preseason starts anyway." He grinned and shook his head. "You're just as gorgeous as ever. How's life? Skeet says you're teaching for Belltown?"

She nodded, shoving her hands into the small pockets of her shorts. "Adjunct professor."

"Oh-ho." He held up an imaginary eyeglass to one eye. "Professor. I say . . ."

"Stop," she groaned, laughing. "It's basically a part-time job. But better than nothing. You're looking good. Great game today, though I'm sorry about the loss."

He shrugged again. "Wasn't a great game, but I did what I could. We've got a lot of new guys, so we're working it out. Not too worried. I can pay up as soon as Skeeter gets out. I feel like pizza. You game?"

Erica nodded. "Pizza works." She looked over towards the locker room. "He should be out soon."

"Before he is, come here." He pulled out his phone and pulled her close. "Smile for the boys, Teach."

She gave a wide-mouth grin with a wave while Ryker merely looked smug, which was kind of hilarious. Ryker was never smug unless it was with the Pack. Even then, it was rare.

"Perfect," he said, fingers flying as he typed. "Jealous replies in three . . . two . . . one . . ."

On cue, his phone dinged, making Erica laugh.

"Axel," Ryker informed her. "He didn't say anything; he just sent three flame emojis." He winked at her. "Probably for me."

"Probably," she agreed.

The locker room door opened, and Sawyer finally came out, hair damp, no bags in sight.

Erica frowned at that.

Sawyer waved as he approached, managing a small smile. "Rabbit, that was a beautiful hit in the fourth. And I hope you pay the guy who washes your uniform after that stunt in the seventh. Ugly stuff, man."

Ryker barked a mock laugh. "Doesn't have to be pretty if it gets the job done. You ready for me to pay up? I'm starving, and Erica wants pizza."

Erica snorted softly. "I'll eat anything."

"You're an exceptional woman," Ryker replied at once before returning his attention to Sawyer. "So?"

Sawyer shocked them both by shaking his head. "Can't tonight, buddy. Got film and meetings. Take Erica, though. It'll count, and she needs dinner."

"I can wait," Erica insisted, coming over to take his hand. "I don't mind."

He shook his head again. "Sorry, babe, it's going to be a late night. Lots of work to do. I'll call you tomorrow, okay?" He gave her a quick kiss and stroked her cheek. "Love you."

"Love you too," Erica murmured as Sawyer pulled back, giving Ryker a fist bump.

"Bring my girl back, Rabbit," Sawyer teased, though there was something forced in it.

Ryker nodded, not joining in the joke. "Sure thing. Later."

Sawyer headed back to the team room, leaving the pair of them alone.

"I don't know what that's about," Erica said softly. "At all."

"Skeet does his own thing," Ryker reminded her. "He'll be all right. Come on, let an old friend feed you."

Erica went with him, but she glanced back towards the team room, not at all convinced.

# CHAPTER 11

"GOOD EYE, SKEET. Nice job."

"Thanks, Sarge. Anything you see that I can improve on?"

Sarge raised a graying brow. "Val says you've been putting in extra time in the cages with Gru. You're already getting pointers."

"I know, but you're the coach." Sawyer shrugged. "You might see different things."

The older man eyed Sawyer with a suspicious glint in his knowing eyes, and he chewed his gum silently. Then he dipped his chin once. "You hesitate before the swing more often than not, gives you a momentary jerk before the motion. Make the decision and execute. Smooth swing, connect, follow through."

Sawyer nodded, pressing the bat into the ground and twisting in thought. "I can see that, right. Okay, thanks, Sarge." He tapped the bat hard, then kicked it up from the ground, swinging it up to his shoulder. "I'll go for a few more. Wanna be ready for LA."

"Skeet, you're done."

No, he wasn't. He had so much more to do, more to improve, more reps to take. There was plenty still to practice and work on, and he pitched again tomorrow. He wouldn't be able to do much in tonight's game; he had to rest up, so this was his last chance to redeem himself and get confidence back. He had to keep working. He had to . . .

"With batting," Sarge went on, looking at Sawyer in confusion. "Head on over to the bullpen for a few reps, okay? Nothing hard. We need you tomorrow."

Sawyer nodded, but he wasn't happy about it as he handed his bat over and jogged over to his cap and mitt. Batting was his biggest weakness on the field, and he needed to improve on that more than anything if he wanted to help out his team. He'd watched hours of film of his batting alone to check what he could improve on, and Gru had been generous with his time and his experience, helping him fine-tune his swing and stance.

If he'd been out of season, he'd have spent hours in the cages, too, taking rep after rep until he could barely lift his arms.

He wanted to push hard, to ache with his efforts, to really feel throughout his body that he was improving.

Most of the time he just felt sluggish these days.

He yawned as he moved over to the bullpen area, where the rest of the pitchers were practicing with their practice catchers, some throwing harder than others, and some having intense discussions with each other about strategy.

"Hey, Skeet!"

Sawyer turned to see Mace jogging over from batting, taking off his helmet and_rolling it towards the dugout, stripping off his batting gloves. Sawyer lifted his chin in greeting.

"Wanna go?" Mace called, smiling wide. "You and me. Show up the rest of the gang, eh?"

"Yeah right, Mace," Indy called. "I can hear your knees creaking from here!"

"Need to take your aspirin first, Mace?" Jesse added as he shook his arm out.

Mace's look turned mischievous. "First one to nine strikes doesn't have to shag balls for a week."

Whistles and low sounds of appreciation raced across the group, and everyone prepped for the challenge.

Sawyer scowled and adjusted his cap as Mace started putting on his gear. "Why would you do that?"

Mace looked up as he attached one leg guard. "Do what?"

He gestured to the line of waiting teammates. "Strike throwdown. Why make this a competition?"

"Because it's fun?" Mace scoffed as he grabbed the other leg guard. "We always do crap like this. What's the big deal?"

Sawyer grunted to himself and shook his head. "Nothing. Just would rather take my reps and work out kinks, not goof off during good practice time."

Mace squatted down, stretching into his position, then rested his forearms on his knees as he held, looking up at Sawyer. "What's got your teeth in a grind? You never miss an opportunity to mess around."

"Not when it interferes with work." Sawyer exhaled, punching gently into his mitt. "There's too much to do. LA is really good, and they owned the Knights yesterday."

"LA?" Mace repeated, slowly straightening and shaking his legs out to loosen them. "That's tomorrow. We've got the Grizzlies tonight."

"So I'm thinking ahead," Sawyer snapped. "I don't pitch tonight, so I'm not that worried about the Grizzlies. I'll let Vandy worry about them, all right?"

Mace stared at Sawyer in silence, then whistled down the line. "Hey Vandy, how you feeling, bro?"

"Feelin' good, Mace!" the pitcher shouted back, swinging his left arm in wide circles.

"Worried about them bears tonight?"

"Nah," Vandy sputtered. "Gonna be fun. Take a nap today, Mace. I'm going with my man Johnny B, all right?"

"Sounds good, man." Mace tilted his head towards them, his eyes on Sawyer. "He sound worried to you?"

Sawyer scowled, pulling his hand out of his glove and working his fingers. "It's not my job to think about Vandy's mental state. If he feels good, that's wonderful. I've got to get my head ready for LA, so I'd appreciate not throwing my arm out in a stupid competition."

His friend put his hands on his hips, his chest protector still on the ground. "Who said anything about throwing your arm out? Nine strikes, that's it. Nobody's throwing that hard right now, not with a game tonight." He stepped towards Sawyer, his brow furrowed. "What's up, huh?"

"Nothing." Sawyer shook his head and shoved his mitt back on. "I'm good. Didn't sleep much."

"I can tell," Mace replied. "You look like hell."

"Nice," Sawyer snapped. "You made a rhyme." He rubbed a hand over his face, exhaling. "Sorry. Been studying film, and studying . . . other stuff . . ."

Mace nodded in understanding, his eyes darting quickly to the others. "Uh-huh, got it. You sure that's all?"

Sawyer nodded, lying with every bob of his head. "Yeah."

"Okay." Mace thumped his arm. "Snap out of it, huh? Nine strikes, Skeet. Get creative, okay?"

Knowing he couldn't get out of it, not if he wanted his teammates to leave him alone, he nodded and turned to the rubber set out for him.

"Come on, boys," J-Rob hollered from his position. "I'm losing power the longer we stand here."

"Yeah, Skeeter, line 'em up!" someone else yelled.

"Great," Sawyer muttered to himself. "Just great."

If it wasn't the Six Pack barking at each other with taunts over their records and ridiculous stats, it was his teammates eying him as though he were supposed to deliver something epic.

Epically awful was more like it. His arm hadn't felt the same since the night he came in for Hanksy, and it terrified him.

He couldn't lose his arm. He couldn't.

He wouldn't.

Nine strikes. He could throw nine strikes without blowing anything; it was just for practice. He'd been throwing the ball nearly every day since he was seven, and he had pitched regularly since he was thirteen. He'd had his rounds with tendinitis, but that was ages ago, and he'd recovered great. He took great care of his arms and never exceeded his max reps. He was a smart player and listened to his body.

Or he thought he did.

At the moment he wasn't entirely sure where most of his body was, but three hours of sleep would do that to a guy.

History of Sport was kicking his tail when he wasn't actually studying his own sport. It was way more involved than he thought it would be, and he was beginning to question everything he thought he knew about sports in general.

Then there was studying his old sports psych notes from college, and his own notes from sessions with Dr. T back at Belltown. They'd all been required to meet with the sports psychologist regularly, and Sawyer had learned a lot from the guy.

He wasn't teamed up with a sports psychologist now, though he probably should be. He'd heard that one of his old teammates had gone into sports psych and was doing really well with it, but he didn't know how he felt about reaching out at this point.

It would just be one more thing for his plate, and he really didn't have space.

Or time.

Nine strikes. He could pitch nine strikes.

He looked down at Mace, waiting for Damien to start them off.

"No rapid fire," Damien instructed. "Clean calls, Catch. Got it?"

All of the catchers grunted in unison.

"Pitch, no more than seventy-five percent. Got it?"

Sawyer and the pitchers acknowledged the instruction with a mixture of grunts and squeals, depending on the current degree of ridiculousness the individual was feeling.

Damien rolled his eyes. "Right. First to nine clean strikes, raise hands. Set. Go."

Sawyer came set, exhaled, and threw, roughly seventy-percent effort on a two-seam.

*Strike.*

A thrill of elation hit his gut, and he acknowledged Mace's nod with one of his own.

He caught the ball, circled the rubber, and looked at Mace again.

Came set. Exhaled. Pitched.

*Ball.*

He gritted his teeth as the ball barely missed the dirt, shaking his head at himself.

Catching the ball, he circled again.

Set. Exhale. Pitch.

*Ball.*

Too wide.

Circle again. Set. Pitch.

*Ball.*

"Dammit," he hissed, catching again.

Circle. Set. Pitch.

*Ball.*

Sawyer shook his head, waving off Mace before he could throw the ball back to him, and strode away from the bullpen, yanking his mitt off his hand, keeping his eyes on the ground.

*Can you come over?*

Erica stared at the text longer than she should have, sitting on her patio in the warm Arizona morning.

There were just too many emotions.

After the horrible game against LA last night, Sawyer had hugged her without a word, holding her for so long she actually thought he might have fallen asleep holding her.

Then he'd said he had to go, and he left without her.

Again.

It was becoming a pattern now, and she hated it. Win or lose, he left the game alone, and so did she. He spent all his time watching film, studying players, and practicing. He never texted her unless it was about schoolwork, of all things, but he never pushed her away either.

He always said there was no time.

He apologized, but he had no time.

For her.

Old fears were resurfacing, as were old feelings and memories she'd rather not have back in her mind. Insecurities that had plagued her senior year of college, swayed her away from teaching, and shaped her life to what it now was returned, and she second-guessed absolutely everything.

She hadn't been ready for this again, but she'd jumped in anyway.

Knowing how baseball took over Sawyer, how lost in his head he became, she'd known instinctively this could happen.

And she had risked it anyway.

She'd barely slept a wink last night, worrying about what that hug from Sawyer had meant. She'd felt love, she'd felt desperation, she'd felt need . . . but there had been something else that scared her. Something that kept her clinging to him as much as he was to her.

Fear. Knee-shaking, heartbreaking fear that something magical was coming to an end.

And now this text.

Was he reaching out to bring her in, or was he simply going to escort her out?

What should she do?

She exhaled slowly, inhaled deeply, and exhaled again.

Her phone buzzed in her hand before she could respond.

*Come over, babe. Please?*

Erica swallowed hard. Heaven help her, she wanted to go to him, no matter what the outcome of all this was. She loved him, in spite of his being lost in his own head, despite his alienating her, and even though he was breaking her heart.

She loved Sawyer Bennett, and he had asked her to come.

Maybe there was hope. Maybe this would end, and they could move forward together.

She smiled and texted out a quick response. *Absolutely. Be right there.*

She pushed out of her chair and dashed into her apartment, changing her clothes and running a brush through her hair. Then she was in her car, heading down to his apartment in Mesa, trying to calm her frantically racing heart.

Before she had fully prepared herself for whatever was coming, she was standing before his door and knocking, suddenly feeling too much like she had when she was sixteen and preparing to ask Danny Little to their high school home-coming dance.

Danny had said no.

She hoped Sawyer wouldn't.

The door swung open, and Sawyer stood there looking as though he'd just come from bed or he desperately needed to go there. Gray Belltown sweats and wrinkled blue Belltown baseball tee, hair in complete disarray, and messy scruff. His eyes were a faded shade of his usual blue, and his smile didn't reach them.

"Hey, beautiful," he murmured, opening an arm hesitantly.

Erica's heart broke a little, and she immediately moved into his arms, squeezing gently. "Hi, handsome."

Sawyer exhaled roughly as he held her, then pressed a kiss to her neck. "I'm sorry."

Her eyes filled with hot tears, and she blinked them away as quickly as she could. "For what?" she quipped sarcastically.

He chuckled against her and pulled back, the smile reaching his eyes this time. "I love you, and I especially love your sarcasm."

She shrugged. "I was born with it. Decided to improve it as I got older."

Sawyer stroked her hair, running a thumb across her cheek. "You did good." His smile faded, and he sighed, searching her eyes.

Erica looped her hands around his waist. "What can I do, Sawyer? What do you need?"

"Can you find my baseball skills?" he asked, trying for the teasing air he usually had. "I used to have them, but I don't know . . ."

"Stop it," she urged softly. "You're okay. A couple of rough games doesn't mean anything."

Sawyer shook his head slowly before she finished. "It's more than that, hon. My head and my heart aren't in it, and I can't seem to figure out what went wrong."

"That's just pressure, babe," Erica insisted, keeping him fixed to her when he gently tried to break away. "Nobody expects you to be both you and Hanks. Jess said they're just going to pull Marty over to starter instead, and that'll work fine. It's a shot for him, and that's good, right?"

"It's great," he assured her, putting his hands on her upper arms. "Fantastic. Marty's great, and he deserves a shot. That's not it." He tried again gently, but very firmly, to separate from her, succeeding this time, and moving over to his windows, folding his fingers behind his head.

The action made his shirt ride up, and the base of his spine and the lower sides of his torso were visible to her. Muscular, trim, attractive . . . She smiled softly, finding it strangely funny that she could notice and appreciate his appearance even when she suddenly felt this horrible sinking feeling in her stomach.

"What happened to Hanksy could easily happen to me," Sawyer admitted, his back still towards her. "Easily. To any pitcher. We know that, every one of us. But seeing it up close, and to a friend . . . It shakes you."

"That's understandable," she murmured as she sank onto the arm of the nearby couch. "Anyone would feel that."

Sawyer shook his head, his hands moving to grip his neck instead. "I'm afraid to pitch, Erica. It's all I know, it's what I do, and I'm afraid to do it."

Erica gaped at him, though he couldn't see it. "Why?"

"Why?" he repeated. He whirled to face her, the exhaustion transformed into a frantic energy. "Because if I go down like Hanks, I don't have a backup. If I lose my arm, I have nothing. I've been up every night studying, finishing assignments, killing myself to make up for the fact that I've completely screwed up my life."

"What? Sawyer, no. You're not going to go down like Hanks. And he's not finished forever; you heard the report yourself. He might be ready before postseason!" Erica got up and came over to him. "Stop, stop. You're exhausted and overworked. You're not thinking clearly."

He ran his hands through his hair, then pressed the heels of his hands into his eyes. "I know. I know, I know, and I realized that about two in the morning." He exhaled shakily. "I've been watching film to improve my game, and I've been doing exercises and treatments with Doc and Kayla to keep my arm healthy. Add to that my schoolwork, and . . ."

"It's too much," Erica whispered, rubbing his arms and pulling his hands from his eyes. "You can't do everything at once, babe. One step at a time, and it'll all come together."

Sawyer nodded, leaning forward to press his lips to her brow. "I need some time."

"Sure you do," she agreed. "There's lots of time."

He slowly shook his head, pulling back to look at Erica more fully. "Erica, I need some time. From us."

Erica's heart stopped in her chest. He didn't want time *with* her. He wanted time *from* her.

"What?" she breathed.

He immediately cupped her face in his hands. "I'm in the middle of a mess, and I don't want to hurt you. I need to focus on untangling it. I need to focus on baseball and get my game back for my team, for my future . . . For *our* future. And for me."

Erica swallowed, blinking. "Why do I feel like I already know this speech?" she asked, not bothering to keep the bitter edge out of her words, wrenching her face out of his hold.

"No, no!" he insisted. "This is different! I love you, I do.

I just can't think right when you're around." He winced even as he said it.

She shook her head, moving back to the couch to grab her purse, sniffling but refusing to let the tears fall while he could see them. "What kind of relationship do you expect us to have if I can't be around?"

"Erica," Sawyer pleaded, and she could see his torment, which only made hers worse. "I don't want to lose you. I just need time."

She managed a pained smile. "Good. I don't want to lose you either. But this feels like I already have." She blinked rapidly and opened the door, letting it slam shut behind her as she hurried to her car, the tears rolling freely down her cheeks.

# CHAPTER 12

"LOOK AT THAT release. What a mess, absolutely no follow-through. What is that?"

The tape skipped forward, and another pitch was analyzed.

"No, no, no . . . You call that a change-up? Disgusting."

Again, the tape moved ahead.

"You've gotta be kidding me. Where do you think the strike zone is? Where?"

There was no answer from the empty team room, and Sawyer didn't expect there to be. He was analyzing his last game, miserable as it had been, and facing every single pitch from that night. He hadn't watched any of the sports coverage on TV this time, not needing to hear from anyone else how horrible his performance had been.

He knew full well.

The last few days, he'd devoted himself to his own analysis, forgoing even his coursework until he could at least get baseball back in his good graces, or get himself in baseball's good graces, whichever the case happened to be. He was careful to only throw the specific number of pitches he was supposed to on his off days, and he did preventative rehabilitation with the athletic training staff daily.

He ran more than he probably should, but running cleared his head.

Well, in theory it did.

His head was so muddled these days he couldn't think straight most of the time, and running tended to get rid of a few snarls here and there.

He'd taken a step out of his usual pattern to sit with the bullpen for a game or two, mostly to work on technique with the others and to chat with Damien about his own pitching and get some ideas for his improvement. Tomorrow he would pitch again, but it was a split-roster game, so he didn't feel the same sense of pressure. His arm felt good, but he hadn't analyzed the details of Arizona's batters yet.

It always tended to ache in anticipation after he did that.

Sawyer looked down at the pages of notes, trying to find a common theme.

There was none.

He rubbed at his eyes and looked over at the clock on the wall. Eleven in the morning, which meant he'd been at this for four hours. The team would be showing up in an hour for warmups before heading out to the game, and he'd already gotten in some good cardio, some weights, and his rehab.

He turned a few pages in his notebook to the schedule he'd laid out for himself. The morning was designated for pitching film, then tonight would be prep for tomorrow's game. He needed to get good sleep the night before he pitched, so he would take that seriously.

He had to.

"Whoa, what's this? No one told me it was movie night."

"It's not even lunch," Sawyer replied, pressing Play on the film again.

Mace grunted. "Right. Let's try that again."

Sawyer didn't look, but he could hear retreating footsteps. "Oh, good, he meant that literally."

The footsteps came back. "Whoa, what's this? No one told me it was movie brunch."

"Probably because you weren't invited," Sawyer replied, watching what was possibly his only good pitch of that game.

Mace came into the team room completely, coming to stand behind Sawyer and watching film for a second. "Oh, I've seen this one. There's a really great play in the seventh, and the guy singing 'Take Me Out to the Ballgame' forgets the words."

"How exciting," Sawyer said dismissively, adding the pitch he'd just watched to the illustration of the strike zone he'd drawn on a page of his notebook.

The two of them watched the next pitch in silence, and Mace chuckled darkly to himself. "I couldn't believe he called that one a ball. It was low, but not *that* low, and I felt the heat. It's been a while since you've pitched that hot, bro."

Sawyer grunted and pressed pause. "Well, it doesn't matter if it didn't count for anything, does it?" He pushed up from his chair and moved over to the lights, flipping them on and squinting faintly against the brightness of them.

Then he really looked around. Remnants of his breakfast sat to one side of his chair, papers that had fallen from his notebook had scattered on the floor, his backpack had tipped over and his textbooks had started to slide out, and the sweatshirt he'd been wearing this morning but removed some time ago lay six feet away, where he'd tossed it.

The place was a sty.

"Uh, wow," Mace said as he took in the whole picture, whistling to himself. "Love what you've done with the place."

"Shut up," Sawyer muttered, picking up the folding chair and putting it back with the others on one side of the room.

"Sorry," Mace replied with a laugh. He gestured around as Sawyer began to tidy up. "What's all this? Were you doing homework?"

Sawyer paused in the process of picking up his backpack. "Something like that."

"Uh-huh." Mace sat down on one of the wide leather couches in the room, crossing his size-seventeen shoe over one knee. "And you got distracted by film? There are better games to watch, if you're wanting to really get distracted."

"Trust me, I'm well aware." Sawyer zipped up his bag, then began picking up the papers. "But watching good games isn't going to help me get out of this mess, and it's not going to help me improve."

"Hold the phone," Mace ordered, his voice turning almost cold. "And back that up. Mess?"

Sawyer gave him a dubious look. "As if you didn't know. As if anyone on the team didn't know."

Mace blinked, his brow furrowed, dark beard hiding his mouth completely. "You're going to have to enlighten the dumb idiot on the couch, Skeet. Spit it out."

"I suddenly suck at baseball," Sawyer reminded him, eyes wide with disbelief. "Can't pitch to save my life. Bat like it's T-ball. It's all they can talk about on ESPN."

"Seriously?" Mace shook his head. "You know better than to watch that after a bad game. That's being judged in the court of public opinion, and you don't need that crap."

Sawyer laughed once, without any humor whatsoever. "Bad game. If only it were just a bad game. How about two completely craptastic games in a row for me? How about two weeks of horrible practices? How about suddenly forgetting how I'm supposed to hold a ball for a two-seam when I could have thrown it blindfolded in my sleep before?"

Mace tilted his head in a question. "Why would you need to be blindfolded if it's in your sleep?"

Sawyer shoved the small stack of papers into his notebook and dropped that on the floor in frustration. "Great. Just great. Go ahead and make a joke out of it. Laugh it up, this is so hilarious."

"Knock it off, Skeet," Mace said, losing his teasing air. "You're reading way too much into bad games, and it's messing with you. This is beneath you."

"Apparently not," Sawyer shot back as he picked the rest of his things up from the floor and moved to set them on the couch opposite the one Mace occupied. "I can't have bad games, Mace. I can't get sent down."

"Whoa, whoa, whoa," Mace insisted. He sat up, holding his hands out like he was calming a wild horse. "Who's talking about sending you down?"

Sawyer dropped himself onto the couch, flopping one leg up onto the cushions and rubbing his hands over his face. "It's only a matter of time, isn't it? Sarge is going to want pitchers who deliver. If Marty does well and Hanksy gets back before postseason, they'll send me back down instead of Marty, and I'll never get out of there. I'll have blown my shot."

"That's not gonna happen," Mace told him firmly. "You're in a rut. It happens, and it happens all the time. You'll get out of it."

"Until I blow out my arm like Hanksy," Sawyer rebutted. "And then I'll be out of commission until I recover, and I may never be like I was before. Not that it would make any difference now. I suck as it is."

"All right, that's it." Mace pushed up from his couch and came to stand before Sawyer. "If you're done with your epic pity party for one, I'd like to talk to my teammate for a second."

Sawyer glared up at him, but nodded once.

Mace folded his arms, looking every inch the intimidating powerhouse he was. "You need to get your head out of

wherever it is and back on your shoulders. This right here"—
he gestured to Sawyer in general—"this can't happen. You're
sabotaging yourself and, by extension, your team. Stop
feeding the spiral. Step back, take a look at everything, and get
back in the game."

"There's no time to step back in preseason," Sawyer
reminded him grumpily, shifting in discomfort.

"I was being metaphorical, moron," Mace snapped. He
exhaled slowly, shaking his head. "What does Erica say?"

Sawyer winced and looked away.

Erica. He missed her so much he couldn't stand it, and
she was only twenty minutes away. He knew he had to do this,
and he knew she hated it. There was no winning here, but he
didn't know what else to do.

"Please tell me you aren't that much of an idiot."

Sawyer swallowed, glancing up. "To do what?"

Mace stared at him with round eyes. "You broke up with
her?"

"No," Sawyer retorted defensively. "No. We just . . . I
just . . ."

"Does Erica know you didn't break up with her?" he
asked. "Or is she just as confused about that as you are about
everything right now?"

Sawyer shook his head. "She knows. I told her I needed
space and time. To focus, to get my head right, to . . . I don't
know. It was harder with her."

"Oh, and you feel so much better now?" Mace scoffed
loudly. "You're so worried about your position on this team,
and not letting the team down, and your performance on this
team, and yet you're forgetting your most important teammate. You're a world-class idiot, Skeet. Fix it."

Mace left the team room before Sawyer could respond to
that statement, but he wasn't sure what he would have said
anyway.

He was an idiot. He was a jerk too, but mostly an idiot. He was rapidly losing control of his carefully juggled life, and struggling to remember how to do anything he once managed so well.

Moderately well, anyway.

He might not be able to get everything squared away perfectly right now, but he could certainly try to make sure he and Erica were okay.

He needed her. He knew that and always had known it.

But what if . . .?

He shook his head and pulled out his phone, texting her quickly before he could talk himself out of it.

*Miss you, babe. Late-night breakfast after the game? Love you.*

She would be at work now, but she would respond eventually.

He could fix this.

He could.

Her bags were packed, and Erica could only stare at them. Blankly.

She was leaving. Strange, Arizona had only been her home for a few weeks, and she'd known that from the beginning, but it now held a special place in her heart.

It had become home.

Sawyer had made it home.

She hadn't seen him in four days. Not since the impromptu late-night breakfast.

The game where he'd been pulled in the fourth inning.

He hadn't texted or called, and he hadn't waited for her after that game or any other game since.

She knew he was reading her texts—she had the read receipts—so he knew she was leaving today.

He still hadn't sent anything.

They hadn't talked about where they stood, what they were, or what happened next. She wasn't the sort of woman to sit and wring her hands over a guy or complain about labels, but she did have just enough self-respect to want clarity in a relationship.

She needed to know if the man she was in love with felt strongly enough about her to make this work between them.

At this moment, she was all of twenty-one years old, back on her mother's back porch, wondering what she had done to make her boyfriend break up with her.

The only difference was that this time he hadn't broken anything up.

Technically.

Her phone buzzed, and she glanced down at the screen.

The car was here to take her to the airport.

Well, that was that, then.

She got up from the couch and glanced around the apartment one last time. Everything had been cleaned, the groceries had been cleared out, and nothing of hers remained.

New York was waiting, and so was her next assignment at the museum.

She wheeled her suitcase out of the apartment and started down the stairs, hauling it awkwardly in front of her, trying in vain to see the stairs before she stepped on them.

It would be too perfect to tumble down the stairs and break something or bruise several things and be forced to stay longer.

Without any hospital visitors.

She shook her head, scolding herself. Sawyer would come if she were injured. Things weren't *that* bad.

Maybe she should fall down the stairs then.

They could talk.

Setting her suitcase back down on its wheels, Erica straightened and brushed a long lock of hair back behind her ear. She hadn't paid much attention to her ponytail when she had thrown her hair back, but she'd evidently need to fix it at some point.

"Hey."

She jerked around towards the parking lot only to see Sawyer leaning against his car, staring at her.

He looked ridiculously good. Miserable, but good. He was in his trademark Belltown sweats and a plain gray fitted tee, and he'd shaved his scruff.

She was glad for that, for some reason.

Erica swallowed hard. "What are you doing here?" she asked weakly.

Sawyer lifted one shoulder in a shrug. "I thought maybe I could take you to the airport."

So he did know she was leaving. He did care that she was leaving.

Would he stop her?

No, he'd just said he wanted to take her to the airport. He was going to help her leave.

He wasn't stopping her at all.

She shook her head. "I'm not sure that's a good idea."

His face tightened at her words. "Erica . . ."

"Sawyer," she said softly, adjusting her purse onto her shoulder. "I'm not leaving you. This isn't me running away. I live in New York, and my assignment here is done. I stretched it as long as I could, and you weren't offering me any reason to stay."

Sawyer's throat worked on a swallow, and he lowered his eyes to his shoes, the toe of one suddenly digging at the pavement. "I know. I'm sorry."

Erica sighed and folded her arms, stepping closer to him.

"You wanted time, and now you get distance too. This will be good. I won't be constantly worrying about you, and you'll get your chance to re-center and focus again."

"I need you," Sawyer admitted with a rawness she hadn't anticipated.

She gave him a pitying look. "Sawyer, I'm a phone call away. And you can text on that phone too, you know." She tried for a smile, but she knew it fell flat.

Sawyer looked as though she had kicked him. "Babe, please . . ."

"Please what, Sawyer?" she cried, losing the control she had forced herself to have. "Please go? Please stay? Please be there, please don't? I don't know what you want me to do. I don't know what I *can* do."

His blue eyes searched hers, so brilliant against the bright Arizona sky. "I don't know either."

Erica nodded slowly, her heart seeming to pound and expand at the same time. "Then it really is best that I go. For now, at least."

He said nothing as he stared back at her, his expression filled with an unspoken intensity. His agony was evident, and she felt it echoing within her.

If she didn't leave soon, she might never be able to.

Exhaling, she closed the distance between them and took his hand. "I love you, Sawyer," she reminded him, her voice catching on the words.

"I love you," he whispered back.

She nodded once more. She knew that; she'd always known that.

It didn't change things, but she knew.

"But," she continued, "you need to figure out what it is you want and where I fit into that. If I do."

His chest expanded with a deep inhale, and she thought

for a moment that he would deny it. Then he surprised her by releasing his breath, his shoulders slumping, and he nodded in agreement, his thumb rubbing absently over her hand.

"I love you," she said one more time, squeezing his hand as tightly as she dared. "Okay?"

"Okay," he replied, his mouth curving to one side just a little. "I'll call you."

Erica somehow managed a weak smile. "You better." She ran her thumb across his briefly, then stepped back and reached for her suitcase.

It was now or never.

She nodded to herself and wheeled her bag to the waiting car without looking at Sawyer.

She'd never make it if she looked at him again.

The driver took her suitcase and loaded it for her while Erica slid into the back seat, closing the door behind her.

Her lungs began to contract on painful breaths, but she forced herself not to break. Not yet. Not while he could see her.

The driver got back into the car and silently fastened his seatbelt, then pulled away from the parking lot.

Against her better judgment, Erica turned to look out of the rear window. Sawyer stood there still, facing her. He saw her and raised his hand to wave at her.

She lifted a hand to wave back, then wrenched herself forward, the pain in her lungs growing more intense by the second.

The car pulled out of the complex and onto the main road, heading towards the airport.

Then, and only then, did Erica burst into tears, burying her face in her hands.

169

# CHAPTER 13

"YOU GOT THIS, Skeeter. Come on, kid, get him."

Sawyer nodded, though Papa Jim wouldn't be able to see it. He wet his fingertips and exhaled.

Circle. Pause. Crack his neck side to side. Exhale and drop the shoulders. Look at third.

Remy nodded at him, looking more serious than Sawyer had seen him in weeks.

He looked at Mace, nodded at the signal, then exhaled.

*Left, left. Right, right. Left, right.*

Come set.

Draw up, cock back, release, follow through.

"Strike!"

Sawyer sighed heavily, relief washing over him. He needed this. He needed this badly.

So far, so good. It was still middle of the fifth inning, so there was a lot of game to play and a lot of balls to pitch, but nothing had been disastrous yet.

*Yet* being the operative word.

He caught the ball from Mace and moved back to the rubber, going through his routine again.

"Eyyyy, Skeeter, here we go, Skeeter!" Remy hollered.

Sawyer looked to Mace, shaking his head twice at the signals, then nodding when he saw the one he wanted and coming set.

He pitched, watching the ball as he followed through.

"Strike!"

He pumped his fist with a jolt of excitement.

"Come on," he told himself, catching the ball again. "Let's go."

Once more he went through the motions and threw, this time the batter getting a piece of it and driving the ball directly to Farrabee, who scooped it up and lobbed it to Papa Jim for the easy out.

"Yes!" Sawyer grunted, pumping his fist again. "Yes, boys!"

Papa Jim whistled and sent the ball to Gru, who sent it to Remy. Remy juggled it for a second, then tossed it up to Sawyer with the yell he usually did when he was excited about something.

Sawyer managed a smile at the sound. Crazy Puerto Rican.

"Two down," Farrabee called, holding up his index and pinky fingers. "End it now."

"Now up to bat, number nine, David McCarthy!"

Sawyer smiled as Grizz did his usual pre-batting action of crossing his arms across his chest and flapping them back and forth before he strode to the plate, tapping his bat against the insides of his cleats. Grizz paused, adjusting his gloves and briefly chatting up Mace.

He always said hi to the catchers.

Weirdo.

Then Grizz looked over at Sawyer, and his grin flashed through his scruffy goatee. He swung the bat lightly, pointing it at Sawyer for just a second.

Sawyer twisted his wrist back and forth, the ball in his hold.

*Left, left. Right, right. Left, right.*

Look.

Mace knew Grizz well. He knew what he could hit and what he couldn't, and he signaled accordingly.

Sawyer nodded and came set, exhaling slowly.

He'd struck out Grizz dozens of times. He could do it again.

He drew up with an inhale, cocked, and released, his breath escaping in a rush.

"Strike!" the ump called.

Sawyer blinked, straightening.

Grizz stepped back, laughing like the maniac he was.

Mace was nodding, though Sawyer couldn't hear anything he said as he tossed the ball back to him.

*Two more. Two more.*

The sounds in Hotchkiss Park faded, and the only sound he could hear was that of his breathing.

*Inhale. Exhale. Inhale. Exhale.*

He scratched the dirt, looked to Mace, shook his head, then nodded.

Came set. Drew up. Released.

"Strike!"

*Inhale. Exhale. Inhale.*

He straightened, nodding to himself, still not hearing anything around him. He caught the ball from Mace and circled the mound again.

One more. Just one more.

Scratch. Look. Nod.

Set. Draw. Release.

"Strike!"

Sound suddenly erupted upon his ears, and he smiled,

exhaling in relief as the crowd and his teammates cheered. He looked at Grizz, who wagged a finger in his direction, still grinning.

Sawyer shrugged at his old friend and tossed him a would-be jaunty salute as he jogged to the dugout.

"Attaboy, Skeeter!" Gru exclaimed as he gave him a high five. "Belltown bet tonight, huh? What are you gonna make Grizz do?"

"Yeah, Skeet!" Remy chimed in as he twirled a batting helmet before setting it on his head. "What's the bet?"

The bet? Sawyer had forgotten all about that. He hadn't planned on anything, but his teammates, Grizz's teammates, and the media would be expecting something.

They knew full well there was that stupid tradition among them, which Sawyer had managed to escape when he'd played Rabbit the other day, as he hadn't been pitching.

Hard to win a bet against a benchwarmer.

Hard to lose one too.

"Not sure," he murmured to his teammates. "I'll think about it."

He didn't need to see the looks on their faces to know that wasn't what they'd expected. He was usually one of the pranksters, and a creative one, but not this time. Not now.

He actually had zero interest in making Grizz do anything. Oh, he was delighted that he'd struck him out, and he knew the Six Pack would be blowing up each other's phones about it, but aside from pitching well, he didn't care.

At all, actually.

He'd given up on everything except baseball since Erica had left, and miraculously, baseball was going better.

Not good, but better.

It wasn't fun, but it was better.

He was delivering for his team tonight rather than

embarrassing them, and there was something to be said for that. He could watch the morning sports reports tomorrow if he wanted to and not be concerned about what they would say. But he wouldn't.

He didn't care.

Erica wouldn't care. She never had. She would have been more excited about his striking out Grizz than about the rest of the night. She would have laughed with him forever about it and goaded Grizz just like one of the guys would have done. She'd have hugged Sawyer just as warmly if he'd lost the game for the team as she would had he won it.

Outcomes didn't matter to Erica.

He did.

Or had.

Would she hear about the strikeout? Would she care now? Would it make her smile?

Would he text her when the game was over?

"Skeet."

He jerked and looked up. "Yeah?"

Papa Jim gave him a look. "You're on deck, bud. Might wanna get up there."

"Right," Sawyer agreed, nodding and taking his cap off. "Right, yeah." He pushed up from the bench and walked over to the stairs, stretching a little as he grabbed a helmet and picked up a bat.

He took a few loosening swings, glancing over at the plate, watching as Creasy dropped a ball just short of the left fielder, making it safely to first without any trouble.

"All right, Skeeter, here we go, kid!" Indy called from the dugout, bringing up some cheers of encouragement from the others.

Sawyer moved to the plate, craning his neck from side to side.

"Hiya, Skeet," Grizz greeted from his position behind the plate. "Nice cutter earlier. She was a beaut."

Sawyer grunted. "Thanks, man."

Grizz frowned behind his mask. "Sup, bro? Your mom okay?"

"Fine," Sawyer told him, scoffing slightly. "Just catch the ball."

"Psst! You're supposed to try to hit it!" Grizz reminded him.

Right. That old thing.

Sawyer swayed himself into position, his bat circling very faintly in the air as he waited.

The pitch came, and he swung at it.

"Strike!"

Sawyer hissed, sliding back a bit and looking up at the top of his bat. "Come on," he muttered.

Grizz said nothing this time as Sawyer prepared for the pitch.

*Too low.*

"Ball!"

That was more like it.

"Nice, Skeet," Grizz murmured from his position.

Sawyer ignored him and waited for the next pitch.

He swung at it, connected, and drove it right to the shortstop, who ended the inning with a double play.

Oh well.

Sawyer ran through first anyway, then circled back, handing his helmet to the coach and moving back to the mound, rubbing a hand over his hair.

Grizz was waiting for him at the mound, mask off, smile in place, holding a fist out.

Sawyer pounded it halfheartedly.

"What's up with you?" Grizz asked through his smile, now clearly fake. "Seriously."

Sawyer shook his head and tilted his head towards the visitors' dugout. "Later. Go."

"Kay," Grizz said shortly with a nod before he jogged back to his team, glancing back at Sawyer.

He ignored that too.

He ignored everything.

For now.

"No, I think it looks great. Might be kind of fun to set up something festive around the holidays, you know? Might get you even more customers."

"Bryant said the same thing."

"He's a smart guy, that brother of mine."

"I heard that."

Erica grinned over at her brother as he looked up from where he was cutting the trunk of what had been the family's Christmas tree that year. They'd let it dry out a lot more than they usually did, but her brother assured her that it would only make for better firewood because of it.

She was convinced he was making it up, but she wasn't going to get into that long-winded discussion. It would only go in circles anyway.

She looked up at the blue sky, dotted with white and gray clouds, and inhaled the fresh air deeply. She loved being back on the farm, the air a mixture of pine, fruit, dirt, and freshly cut hay, and it gave her the warmest feelings of home. It just felt good, and there was no other way to describe it.

A weekend back at home after the whirlwind of Arizona was just what she needed, and she was only too grateful that the museum had let her have time away for it.

Returning to work hadn't been good. Oh, they were delighted by the work she had accomplished with the exhibit in Arizona, and everything had arrived in the shipment perfectly pristine, but there had been no plans for her to take on another assignment when she returned. She would just be back into the regular monotony of the museum, and Erica was the sort of person that needed a project. Or a challenge, at least.

All she had at the moment were her classes.

Those were going well enough, and she had been able to spend more time uploading lectures and doing some videos to give additional information. Assignments were rolling in, and she was getting them back out in record time. The forums had been active enough, and she'd been able to chime in a few times now that her workload was lessened.

And now that her personal life was boring.

She hadn't heard from Sawyer. At all. To be fair, she hadn't reached out to him either. She didn't know how. What to say, if she should say anything, what he would want or need from her . . .

It was like they weren't even together, and that scared her most of all.

She'd been following his games and his numbers and had been pleased to see things improving for him, but there had been some moments of doubt.

He was playing better now that she was gone.

Just like he had at Belltown.

Thankfully, her better sense kicked in, and she reminded herself that she had nothing to do with Sawyer's ability to play baseball. She had respected his every boundary and had been nothing but supportive. He had played well before they had gotten back together, and he had played well while they were together.

The only change had come when Hanks had been injured and Sawyer had needed to refocus.

Maybe now he had.

Then why hadn't he called her?

"Erica."

She turned towards the house, where her mom stood on the porch waving at her. She waved back.

Her mom laughed and waved again. "No, silly, come over here. I need some help with the pies."

"Since I'm so good at that," Erica muttered to her dad and brother.

Bryant laughed loudly. "Have fun, sis. Don't ruin anything we can sell."

She stuck her tongue out at him as she headed towards the house, though he really did have a point.

Their mother was the one gifted with pastry. Erica hadn't inherited that gene, and she hadn't put in enough effort to learn the skill appropriately.

This wasn't a chance to help her mother with the pies themselves.

Her mother wanted to talk.

Erica smiled as she walked into the house—really almost a log cabin in its appearance—and the spacious front room, the kitchen sprawled across the back of the house but entirely visible. She took off her scarf and unzipped her quilted vest, shrugging that off and hanging it on the hook by the door. "Okay, Mom, I'm here," she called as she stepped out of her boots.

"Oh good! Hurry back here. I really need you."

She rolled her eyes and walked towards the kitchen, pausing to scratch the ears of their old basset hound, Sammie. The dog moaned groggily in response, making her smile. She moved into the much warmer kitchen, eying the dozen pies on the table. "Wow, Mom," she murmured. "You have a bake sale coming up?"

Her mother, currently in the process of removing another pie from the oven, gave her a look, closing the oven door with her hip. "As a matter of fact, yes. Kennedy High is having one, and they asked if I would mind donating."

Erica gestured to the table. "A dozen pies? Is anyone else donating, or just Moore Farms?"

"Erica Anne," her mother scolded playfully. "Only four are going to the school, considering I don't have a student there anymore. The rest are for the farmers' market tomorrow. We sold out last week, and I don't want to do that again."

"Makes sense to me." Erica leaned against one of the chairs, watching as her mom placed the fresh pie on the table with the others. "So what am I doing to help?"

"Make up some boxes for the cooler ones, will you?" Her mother smiled pleadingly, batting her eyes in a teasing way.

Erica laughed and walked over to the pile of boxes waiting to be assembled. "Just for you, Mom. And I like the new design, by the way."

Her mother hummed as she returned to the counter, where yet another pie was nearly ready for the oven. "Your sister came up with it. I don't know why the simple berry-and-evergreen pattern bothered her, but it did. This doesn't seem *that* much different, but what do I know?"

"Meg has very particular tastes," Erica pointed out, sitting in a chair and beginning to assemble one of the boxes. "No doubt she'll make over the website too."

"Oh, she is," her mom laughed. "That's been her wish all winter, and now that the tree sales are done, she has time."

Erica widened her eyes meaningfully but said nothing.

"How was Arizona, sweetie?" her mother asked, her voice much softer and more tentative. "You've barely said a word about it."

"Warm," Erica told her, focusing on the lid of the box.

"The museum was really cool, though. Beautiful exhibits and artifacts. They designed the museum itself like a lot of the art. Very cultural, and it absolutely fits in with the surrounding area. And the people that worked there were so awesome. Lots of locals who know the traditions for themselves."

Her mom nodded, laying the top layer of pie crust carefully over the filling. "Good, I'm so glad. I wasn't asking about work, though."

That Erica already knew, but she wasn't going to offer that information up without a fight.

"Oh, the food out there is amazing," she gushed as if that were what her mom was looking for. "Seriously, I may never be able to go back to Mexican food outside of Arizona ever again. Totally not the same. I should have picked up some local recipes for you to try, but I didn't think of it, I'm sorry."

"That would have been great." Her mom continued to nod as she pinched the edges of the pie. "Still not what I want to know."

Erica sighed with reluctance, setting aside her first completed box. "Well, Mom, you're going to have to be very direct about what you're looking for, then. I'm not a mind reader."

"No, but you're also not oblivious," came the reply, just as direct, but gently bestowed.

That was also true, but it didn't change the issue.

Silence filled the kitchen but for the sounds of a turning pie pan on a counter and the folding of paper boxes.

"I see Sally Bennett almost every Saturday at the market, you know," her mom informed her, now tracing a pattern on the top surface of the pie with a knife. "I know more than you think."

"I suspected as much," Erica murmured, folding her next box. "There are no secrets in Belltown."

That earned her a look. "Don't be bitter about this. We're not gossiping about our kids to the entire market."

Erica nodded once. "I know. I just don't want to talk about it."

"About Sawyer?" her mom pressed. "Or about your leaving Arizona without him?"

"Both."

Her mom waited, pretending to look over the pie carefully.

There was no avoiding this, and it would be better to get it over with.

"Sawyer is wonderful," Erica admitted at last, sighing with longing this time. "He's just as funny and charming and sweet as he was in college, only he's more mature. Just as good-looking too. It was so easy to pick up as if no time had passed, and it all happened so fast. I fell so hard so fast, Mom. And then . . . I don't know, he got caught up in his head about too many things, and I got dropped." She frowned, shaking her head. "No, that's not right. He loves me, I can see that, and I know it. He's just lost, Mom, and he won't let anyone help him. Especially me."

The oven opened, and Erica watched as her mom slid the next pie in with ease, shutting the door and setting the time. "Well," her mom said as she turned back to her, taking an open seat, "I imagine it's been hard for him to come into real adulthood without his dad. Charlie understood Sawyer so well and was very much his mental coach, if you remember. Never tried to advise him on baseball, but kept his head on straight. When he lost that coach, he must have felt he was all on his own. Maybe he wasn't ready for that."

Erica hadn't remembered that, as it happened. She had spent so much time wrapped up in Sawyer himself that the supporting characters in the picture were a bit blurred in recollection.

She hadn't thought about Charlie in years, but with the reminder came faded memories. Sawyer looked almost exactly like his dad except for his eyes, which were exactly like his mother's. Charlie had been a calm man, but with an impeccable sense of humor. He wasn't easily riled but was quick to celebrate even the smallest victories.

It would be a poignant loss for anyone to have such a person disappear from their life.

For someone with a position and demands like Sawyer, it could be devastating.

Her heart ached a little more for the man she loved, and it took all of her strength and conviction to avoid pulling out her phone to call him right at that moment.

"I miss Sawyer, Mom," she whispered, the box folding growing more difficult as her eyes filled with tears.

A warm hand reached across the table, covering hers. "I know, sweetheart. And I know how happy he can make you. I won't tell you what to do, and in this, I can't. You have to listen to your heart here, and sometimes that seems impossible. As much as you want to take care of him, make sure you take care of yourself as well." Her mom smiled very gently, the quintessential loving-mother smile that never failed to encourage more tears. "It sounds to me like you both might need each other, if you can figure this all out."

"Would you like to tell him that?" Erica managed to laugh, wiping at her eyes.

Her mom grinned and winked. "Pretty sure he's figuring that out now. But if he takes too long, I'll put a call in to Sally or Rachel. They can make some noise for you."

Erica laughed harder and sat back, letting her hand slide out from under her mother's and returning to her box. "Make some noise. You know, I think the two of them could make a lot of noise for Sawyer, if they put their minds to it. He might actually hate me for siccing them on him."

"I'm quite sure he'd forgive you," her mom assured her. "And pretty darn quickly too."

Erica wasn't so sure.

She wasn't sure about anything anymore.

Her phone buzzed in her pocket, and she jumped, fishing it out of her back pocket. She looked at the screen in disbelief, blinked once, then pushed up from the table quickly and moved to the sliding glass door of the great room as she hit the Answer Call button. "Mace? What's happened? What's wrong?"

# CHAPTER 14

"THE SIX PACK had an amazing week, John. All across the board, no exceptions."

"They really did, Dan, and that's saying something with the Knights."

"The Knights were a mess; there is no question there. How this team got to the World Series last year is beyond me."

"True wild card, that's for sure. And when you trade your top three infielders for draft picks, you're destined to have a slump."

"Grizz McCarthy saved this game, John. Hands down. Even his old buddy Ryker Stone couldn't get home safe and clean, but it was a close call."

"Close calls at the Black Racers' game, too. Sawyer Bennett coming back into baseball, ladies and gents. I mean, look at this catch, right off the bat of Gavin Lyons, and quick shot to Jim Calvin at first. Boom, boom, two outs down. Welcome back, Skeeter."

The TV winked off, and Sawyer stared at the screen where last night's game highlights had just been. They would undoubtedly go on to talk about the other games the Six Pack had, but he had no interest in going over those. He'd barely wanted to hear about his own game, but curiosity had gotten the best of him.

He was back in the good graces of the sports world.

Hooray.

That just left the rest of his life to figure out. Baseball, when he stopped thinking about it, was all muscle memory. He knew how to zone in enough to perform, but without any real motivation behind his own performance, everything was instinct and habit. He didn't need to outshine anyone, and he didn't need to prove anything. He needed to meet the level of his teammates and keep the game moving.

That was it.

He could do that. He'd done that his entire life.

It wasn't fun, but it would do.

Last night he'd even ventured into the online forum for his Museums and Culture class to check out new assignments and discussions.

He'd lasted only five minutes.

Erica was getting more involved in discussions and suggestions, taking a more active role in the coursework with her students. It didn't surprise him one bit. She had always been more of a hands-on instructor, and if she had been given the real platform of a campus classroom, she would have been an extraordinary professor.

She was already the most active online professor he'd ever had.

For the fiftieth time in two days, he fiddled with his phone, toying with the idea of texting her.

He wouldn't do it. He hadn't yet.

He didn't know how.

How could he apologize for letting her leave? How was he supposed to explain just how much of an idiot he was? How did anyone find the words to describe to the person they loved that life was less livable when they were gone?

Not impossible. Not unbearable. Just less livable.

Nothing was fun anymore.

He couldn't even bring himself to pretend to enjoy the group text with the Six Pack, much as that usually amused him. His teammates were leaving him alone, which was great, and he was able to quietly go about his routines, rehab, and life without much interruption.

Routine, monotony, and boredom.

That was his life now.

The most exciting thing that had happened to him this week had been finally reaching the baseball chapters in his History of Sport textbook, when he'd decided to delve back into any educational pursuits that didn't involve his estranged girlfriend.

Was she estranged? Did it count as estranged if he'd been the one to completely neglect their relationship? When she was the one giving everything and he'd barely even existed, wasn't he the estranged one?

Could only one of them be estranged?

It was a ridiculous series of questions, but it wasn't the first time he'd asked them. Nothing in his life seemed to work right now except baseball, and he wasn't sure it counted as working when he was just going through the motions.

Especially when he'd pushed her away for the sake of baseball.

Again.

There was no making up for that. There was no coming back from that. There was absolutely no way in the world he could make her see that she was first priority when he had clearly made her less than that.

He'd have to take an Incomplete in her course. There was

no way he could actually finish it while she was the instructor, not like this. He had no doubt she would grade his work fairly and according to whatever rubric she needed to, but he couldn't do it. Every assignment and exam would remind him of her, and he'd wind up imagining her grading it and wondering if she missed him or if she had to remind herself of her code of ethics to avoid failing him outright.

They'd left things so unclear when she went back to New York, and that had been his fault. He couldn't bear to give it a name, to question it, or to even try to define it. She'd said she loved him even as she got into the car.

How could she when he'd given her no reason to stay?

Even if she couldn't have stayed, he could have given her a reason to consider it.

He'd practically put her on the plane himself.

For all that he'd told her this was different and assured her that he was not the man he'd been in college, he had done exactly the same thing and possibly inflicted even more damage. He had followed the same damaging pattern, the inclination to shut everyone and everything out and avoid facing whatever truth was in front of him.

What a winner he was.

Welcome back, Skeeter, indeed.

The phone in his hand vibrated, and he waited a moment before even turning it over.

Did he want to know? Did he care enough?

He finally turned it over, then frowned and pressed the answer button. "Hello?"

He sat up at once. "Really? What are you . . .? Yeah, sure. I know it, yeah. Okay, give me ten. See ya."

He hung up and stared at the phone again. What were the odds?

Ten minutes later, he was sitting in a booth in Casa Dea,

a diner-slash-Mexican-themed place near the airport, tapping his phone almost anxiously against the table.

"Hey, Sawyer, thanks for meeting me."

Sawyer looked up and rose to his feet at once. "Todd. Yeah, no problem. Glad I was free."

The older man smiled and removed his jacket, which amused Sawyer, given that it was Arizona and at least seventy-three degrees outside. "Me too. Wish I had more time so I could actually catch a game, but working with airlines kinda restricts me to airport meetings only, and I have to hit up Dallas before I can get back home."

"Yikes," Sawyer murmured as he slid back into the booth, wondering if he should remove his cap. What was the protocol for dining with your mother's boyfriend? No one had ever told him the rules here.

Todd took a seat and pulled out the menu. "I've heard the omelets here are phenomenal. The question is which one . . . Or two . . ."

Sawyer grinned and eyed the menu himself. This was a guy he could relate with, no question. "Well, don't ask me for halfsies. I'm not sharing."

"Please," Todd scoffed, raising his eyes from the menu to look at him. "Half. My daughters aren't here, and neither is your mother. I can pound two."

"Okay, go ahead. No judging." Sawyer smiled at the young waitress as she came over and gave his order, and Todd did wind up getting two omelets, though time would tell if he would actually finish both.

Sawyer might actually judge the man if he didn't.

Once they ordered and the waitress left, Sawyer sat back, staring at Todd without shame, and Todd stared back.

After a minute, Todd smiled. "Who's going to blink first, Sawyer? My eyes are going to water soon."

Sawyer chuckled and held up his hands in surrender. "Sorry, man. Sorry. I just . . . Why are you here? I get that you had business, but come on. What's up?"

Todd's smile spread briefly. "Oh, I didn't fool you, huh?"

"Not even a little bit." Sawyer shook his head firmly. "Come on, what's going on? Did Mom tell you to come check on me?"

"Of course," Todd answered, snorting softly. "She's convinced you're not eating and avoiding talking to her and probably falling off the edge of the planet."

Sawyer's mouth curved. That sounded like his mom all right.

"But I wanted to see you, too," Todd continued, leaning his folded arms on the table. "We don't really know each other, and I regret that. Particularly since I'm crazy about your mom."

"Well," Sawyer said with a nod, "anybody who can honestly tell me they're crazy about my mom is already in my good books, so that's a good start. And you're a Belltown man, which also boosts your scores. And then there's your girls . . ."

Todd grinned, then nodded like the proud father he was. "I knew we raised them right for a reason." He sobered just a little. "Though I can put most of that credit on their mother." He laughed to himself suddenly. "If you ever went to one of Tara's soccer games, you'd have heard her. She whistled louder than anyone I've ever met."

"No way, that was her?" Sawyer laughed as well. "Man, that was always epic. She came to a couple of our games, and that whistle was legendary."

"Yeah, she was passionate about Belltown." Todd exhaled softly, still smiling. "It's never really easier, you know. Being without them. Just different. You get used to it, as horrible as it sounds, and it becomes part of you. But there's always a sense that something's missing. Like when you forget to wear your watch one day and everything feels off."

Sawyer looked at Todd with interest, finding a sudden kinship and understanding there. "I know the feeling. Hate it." He cleared his throat as his sudden feelings about Erica came to the surface. "So does my mom make that better?"

Todd nodded, his expression warming. "Yeah. Doesn't take it away completely, and I don't take it away for her. We've talked about that in depth. I'm always going to miss Sarah, and she's always going to miss Charlie. But we feel better together. And we would like to continue to do so for a long time."

The mention of his dad made Sawyer surprisingly emotional, but he didn't miss the hesitation in Todd's voice as he finished. "You . . . what?"

"I'd like to ask your mom to marry me, Sawyer," Todd told him, straightening slightly. "I wanted to ask for your blessing before I do anything. We've talked about it, but I haven't asked her yet. I think it would mean a lot if she knew you were okay with it."

Sawyer blinked, momentarily without words. "Whoa . . . This is . . ." He cleared his throat again and looked down for a second, then met Todd's eyes again. "Do you love my mom, Todd?"

He nodded. "Very much."

"Why?"

"Why?" Todd repeated, a crease appearing between his brows. "Why is an interesting question. Hard to describe. Because she makes me laugh so hard I cry. Because it feels perfect to hold her hand. Because she paints her face when we go to Belltown games. Because she looks just as good in sweats as she does when we go out. Because everything makes more sense with her. Because I'm better with her. Because she's everything."

Sawyer felt himself smiling, and he felt a coil of tension in his gut slowly ease. "I've never heard it like that," he murmured. "But it makes more sense than anything I've heard." He inhaled, then exhaled roughly. "Yes, Todd Landers, I give you my blessing to marry my mom. And I think my dad would want you to be the next guy for her."

Todd grinned outright and reached his hand across the table to shake Sawyer's. "Thanks, Sawyer. That means so much. I can't even tell you. I promise I'll take care of her."

"I know you will," Sawyer replied, gripping the handshake hard. "And I don't think she'll give you much of a choice, if I know my mom."

The waitress appeared with their omelets then, breaking the moment.

"Now time for victory or death by omelets . . ." Todd said as he tucked a napkin into the neck of his shirt. "Not a word to your mother."

Sawyer crossed his heart with his fork. "Not a word. Good luck." He smiled at the man who would soon be his stepfather and wondered, faintly, if he could find a way to be better too.

Somehow.

"This is insane. This is absolutely insane."

"Stop saying that; it isn't insane."

Erica looked up at the bearded duo escorting her dubiously. "It *is* insane, and you two ganging up on me doesn't make it any easier."

Mace and Grizz shared a look. "I have no idea what you're talking about," Mace said in a poor attempt at a nonchalant tone.

"Me neither," Grizz recited blandly. Then he winked at her. "Come on, Erica, you know this is right."

She sighed reluctantly. "Yeah, I know. Doesn't make it less insane." She stopped as they reached the door, and she faced them, eying Mace first. "You sure he's alone?"

Mace nodded. "Positive."

"Okay." She looked at Grizz next. "Promise you'll kill him if I run out crying?"

Grizz raised a hand somberly. "On my honor. And then I'll bring him back to life so the other guys can kill him, too."

"Perfect." She smiled and nodded, then turned to the door, exhaled a shaky breath, and walked into the now-empty Black Racers team room.

Well, almost empty.

Sawyer sat in a folding chair to one side of the room, remnants of a celebration of sorts on the floor of the room, a few hand towels and water bottles also dotting the scene. Sawyer was freshly showered but lost in thought, his game bag on the floor next to him, his hands absently turning his cell phone over and over in his hands.

"Must have been some party," Erica said, shoving her hands into her pockets. "Did you jump out of the cake?"

Sawyer's hands stilled, and slowly his head rose, his eyes wide as he stared at her, disbelief etched in every pore. "Erica?"

Her heart lurched at the almost-whisper, and she managed a smile. "You're looking a little roughed up, Sawyer. Maybe you were the piñata instead."

He managed a very weak laugh. "I feel a little like a piñata right now. What are you doing here?"

"Grizz sent me," she replied. Then she rolled her eyes. "And Mace. They're worried about you. Say you're not yourself. So they double-teamed me while I was home. FaceTime with two scary pro catchers." She curved her lips to one side. "Try explaining that one to my mother."

"Why did they call you?" Sawyer asked, not taking the bait of her joke.

Erica lifted a shoulder. "They think I can help you. I know better."

Sawyer swallowed roughly. "So do I." He blinked hard and looked down. "Believe me, so do I."

Erica hesitated just a moment, then slowly walked towards him. "You're lost, Sawyer. You're trapped in your own head. No one can get you out but you."

"I know," he murmured. "I'm trying." He looked up at her, his hands turning his phone over again. "I'm so sorry, Erica. I'm sorry I didn't ask you to stay. I'm sorry I didn't give you a reason to. I'm sorry that..." He shook his head. "I don't have an excuse. Not one."

Erica took another step towards him. "Sawyer, I don't need an excuse. I don't."

"But you deserve an explanation, and I can't . . ." He grunted and held up his phone, the screen showing an airline-ticket receipt. "I literally just booked a flight to come see you. To try and explain, though I hadn't figured that out yet myself, and to beg for your forgiveness." He swallowed and lowered the phone. "And to beg you to come back with me, if I could manage the other two parts without screwing up."

He had been coming to her? To ask her back?

Her heart leaped into her throat, awkwardly tap-dancing there for a minute while she tried to process. "I'll walk with you every step of the way to get you out of this funk, if you'll let me," she promised, fighting the urge to run at him. "But you have to take that first step. Remember what your dad used to say? The only way out is through. Find your path, find the way."

Sawyer's jaw tightened, and a tight smile formed. "Yeah, I remember. But I'm honestly not sure what the way is here. I've thought about what Dad would say, but . . ."

She took pity on him and set her purse down on the

nearest couch, coming even closer. "Well, for starters, I think we need to reset that head of yours with something completely unrelated to baseball. Maybe a movie? Something that makes you laugh, I think. Then you're getting some decent sleep, and since tomorrow there is no game, you get to actually take the day."

"Still have practice," he reminded her, his smile becoming more relaxed.

"Yes, and Mace is handling that aspect of things." She quirked her brows, grinning at him. "You and the other pitchers and the catchers are doing something different, and I have no idea what he and Coach Damien are up to."

Sawyer shuddered dramatically. "That's a frightening thought."

Erica laughed, tilting her head at him, warming to this exchange more and more. "And I'm going to sit in my seat in the stands for the rest of the preseason, and most of the regular season, meet you after every game, and keep you on task with your classes so we can get you that degree. You won't lose the connection to your dad—you'll enhance it. I promise, you'll feel that."

"Why?" Sawyer asked her, his eyes bright and intense as they held her gaze. "Why are you going to do all of this for me?"

"Because Grizz said he'd buy me a new four wheeler for the farm if I did."

Sawyer tossed his head back on a throaty laugh, and his look turned adoring, making the arches of her feet tingle.

Erica bit her lip, shrugging a shoulder. "Because I still love you, idiot. That's not going to change. So will you please stop cutting me loose? It's getting old."

He slowly rose, his smile curving crookedly, and then opened his arms.

She was to him in an instant, her arms clenching around him, her hands fisting in his shirt. His hold on her was tight and almost cradling.

In that moment, she couldn't have said if she was holding him or he was holding her.

She wasn't sure it mattered.

"I love you so much, Erica Moore," he murmured against the suddenly burning skin of her ear. "I'd ask you to marry me if I weren't a complete headcase right now."

She laughed and arched into him, putting her mouth next to his ear. "Well, we'll work on the headcase part and then you can ask me. And if you ask me nicely, I'll probably say yes."

He reared back. "Probably?" he demanded.

She shrugged again. "You never know. Grizz might ask me first."

Sawyer kissed her hard then, effectively shutting her up, and she was more than willing to end the conversation like that. His lips were insistent and warm, wringing pleasure after pleasure from her, giving as much as taking, and she felt herself spiraling almost deliriously into the delight that was Sawyer Bennett.

"I missed you so much," he whispered against her mouth, grazing against her. "So much."

"I missed you too," she told him, laying a hand along his cheek and smiling. "I missed this."

He smiled back and kissed her quickly. "This is the best." He frowned a little. "How are you actually here? What about the museum? They aren't going to let you off that long."

Erica grinned and looped her arms around Sawyer's neck. "I decided it was time I live a little and listen to my heart. Well, the part that wasn't already running back here to you. So I left my job at the museum."

Sawyer gaped. "You did what? Babe . . ."

"Listen," she insisted with a laugh. "I didn't do it to come running back to you, although it was a perk. I had a better offer. Belltown likes what I've been doing with the classes, and I had some great recommendations from the other universities I've been adjunct for. They've invited me to continue online teaching but in a new program they're developing for people just like you who want to finish their degrees but aren't at Belltown anymore. Mostly online stuff, but I'll be loosely based at Belltown as a full-time employee. The only stipulation is that I get an advanced degree in one of their education programs to qualify for promotion and official professorship, and I'll only have to pay half tuition to do it. I can be a teacher, Sawyer, and not just part-time."

"And a Belltown one at that!" He whooped and picked her up, swinging her around and around, laughing with her. "Oh, babe, this is the best! You deserve this, every bit of it. You know what this calls for."

She pulled back, grinning already. "Sure do."

On cue, they threw their heads back and bellowed, "TIMBERRRRRRRRR!"

Erica squeezed her eyes shut, exhilaration soaring through her. "Gosh, this feels good, doesn't it?"

Sawyer lowered her to the ground, his hand running over her hair, bringing her attention back to him. His thumb ran over her lips gently, and he nodded. "Yeah. Yeah, babe, this feels really good. It feels perfect. It's everything."

Then he leaned down and gently, but firmly, kissed her again.

# EPILOGUE

THE FIREWORKS WERE still going and probably would be for some time, given what had just happened.

No one had expected the Black Racers to beat the Mustangs, and they especially had not expected a three-game sweep.

Their postseason chances had been looking good as it was, but now? Things could only go up.

And Sawyer needed to find Erica, and he needed to find her now.

He searched over the heads of the other family members and friends hanging around the clubhouse, many of whom thumped him on the arms or back. He'd pitched one of the best games of his life, and Jesse had closed the game brilliantly. The Six Pack would be all over his phone shortly, if they weren't already.

The onslaught of messages could wait.

His girlfriend came first.

He saw her then, decked out in her Black Racers gear—his jersey and cap—her smile as wide as humanly possible, her eyes barely visible.

Gosh, she was stunning.

She squealed as he neared and ran to him, jumping into his arms and letting him swing her around. "Babe! Holy cow, that was amazing!"

He laughed and set her down, kissing her hard. "I couldn't have done it without you. Not a single pitch, baby. That was all you."

Erica slugged him in the arm impatiently. "Shut up! That was you and your raw talent and training, Skeet!" She hugged him again. "Ugh, I'm so proud of you!"

Sawyer chuckled, kissing the top of her head. "Thanks, sweetheart." He cleared his throat and picked up the bag he had dropped, slinging it over his shoulder as he wrapped his free arm around her waist, leading them both out of the park. "All right, tonight we are celebrating. We are going all out and seeing Columbus, Ohio in a whole new way . . ."

"Huh-uh, History of Sport exam," she insisted, jabbing a rather pointy finger into his ribs. "You promised."

He coughed in surprise. "Not tonight! Babe, this is a huge win!"

"Immense," she agreed. "Massive. Incredible! And it's August. We had a deal. Call for pizza; we've got a study date."

Sawyer scowled, tugging Erica a little closer. "If only I had a fiancée to talk some sense into my tutor."

Erica sputtered impatiently. "Set up a meeting when you get one, and I'll explain myself to her."

He winced. "Pity I can't propose over pizza and actually tell that story with any pride later."

"Your problem, not mine," she quipped with a shrug.

"Guess I'll have to come up with something else."

"Guess so."

"Something unexpected."

She nodded. "Usually works best."

"Great." He dropped his bag, stopping just out front of the best view of Crossroads Park, and turned to kiss her, taking great care to be gentle but thorough.

Erica looked up at him, a little dazed as he broke off. "Whoa," she breathed. "What was . . .?"

"I love you," he told her without any fanfare. "I'm better with you. I'm everything with you and nothing without you. You bring out the best in me and aren't afraid of the worst in me. You are the friend, partner, and teammate that I want with me through everything, good and bad. Every moment, every minute, for the rest of our lives."

He swallowed hard and bent to take one knee, pulling out of his pocket the ring box he'd been carrying around for a month. "Will you marry me, Erica Moore?"

Erica stared at him, then at the ring, then at him, her mouth hanging wide open. "Sawyer?" she gasped.

He quirked his brows, grinning. "I told you I would, and you said probably . . ."

She managed a weak laugh. "I remember."

"So?" He held the ring up a little further. "Will you?"

She laughed again, this time through tears. "Yeah. Yeah, I will. I'd love to."

Sawyer jumped to his feet and slid the ring onto her finger, his hands shaking as he did so. "I love you, sweetheart," he whispered as he looked back into her eyes.

Erica wiped away a tear, smiling up at him. "I love you too."

He kissed her softly, then pulled her into his arms, exhaling with more relief than he'd thought possible to feel.

Now life was perfect.

Absolutely perfect.

Well . . .

He broke away from her, holding up a finger, grinning with excitement.

201

"Oh no," she moaned. "What are you . . .?"

He whirled around, cupped his hands over his mouth, and bellowed, "TIMBERLINE!"

With perfect timing, the entire Six Pack sprang out from behind cars and bushes just in front of them, yelling in scattered unison, "HEAVE-HO!"

Erica shrieked, her hands flying to her mouth. "WHAT?" she cried, practically dancing where she stood. "None of you are supposed to be here. You all have games!"

Axel grinned as he stepped over the chain, coming over for a hug, the others following. "And Big Dawg has a private plane courtesy of Daddy, so we borrowed it! No sweat, Teach, we'll be back before anyone knows we left!"

"Yeah," Cole snorted, giving her a bear hug. "You think we'd miss this?"

"No way, Teach," Levi echoed with a high five and a hug. "No freaking way."

Grizz and Ryker hugged her too, and the whole Pack pounded on Sawyer in congratulations, which he accepted with gusto.

"I can't believe this," Erica exclaimed, shaking her head. "I just can't believe it!"

"What?" Grizz demanded. "That we're here or that you actually agreed to marry Skeeter? Cuz I can't believe that one myself."

Sawyer hissed and slugged his friend in the arm.

"Eyyyy Skeeter, epically romantic, man!" Remy called as he skipped forward from where he'd evidently watched by the entrance.

Sawyer rolled his eyes and waved at his teammate. "Can it, Remy."

Remy snickered, then turned to the Pack with a huge grin. "SIX PACK! Got room for a seventh, boys? I know all the cheers!"

A loud whistle turned Sawyer back to the park, and he saw Mace and Jess walking out, arms around each other. Mace held a fist up in the air. "She say yes?"

Erica flashed her ring in the lights of the stadium. "I said yes!"

Mace released another more suggestive whistle. "Yeah, baby! Party it up! We got you guys Sunday night, okay? See you, lovebirds!" A few more fireworks went off, and Mace laughed loudly. "Nice touch, Skeet!"

Sawyer laughed, shaking his head. "If only I were that creative."

"Oh, stop," Erica scolded with a slap to his chest. "It was perfect."

He turned to her, pulling her close and grinning. "You're perfect, you know that?"

"Hardly," she corrected with a snort.

"Mmm, pretty close," he insisted. "Guys?"

They all nodded and agreed with varying answers, making them both laugh. "See?" Sawyer told her. "Consensus reigns."

"Never let it be said that the Six Pack was wrong," Erica drawled, slipping her arms around his waist.

"It never has been said," he assured her pompously. "Never will be."

"Of course not," she agreed with a nod.

"The world would end."

"It would."

"Belltown would crumble."

"We can't have that."

Sawyer grinned down at the woman he loved, the one he adored, and he marveled at his good fortune. "Hail to Belltown," he murmured, leaning close.

"And down they go," Erica replied softly, arching up to kiss him.

The Six Pack whooped and hollered their approval.

And were adamantly ignored

# ACKNOWLEDGMENTS

None of this would have been possible without the expertise and wisdom of my brother, Chris. A true lover of baseball, a nerd in its details, and an incredible resource for the slightly less educated fans like myself. I promise this book is not about you, but someday maybe you can be my cover model and make your real dreams come true. Just for you: GO CUBS GO!

# More #BellTown Six Pack Novels

Rebecca Connolly writes romances, both period and contemporary, because she absolutely loves a good love story. She has been creating stories since childhood, and there are home videos to prove it! She started writing them down in elementary school and has never looked back. She currently lives in Indiana, spends every spare moment away from her day job absorbed in her writing, and is a hot cocoa addict.

Visit her online: RebeccaConnolly.com

Made in the USA
San Bernardino, CA
25 January 2019